About Jackie Braun

Jackie Braun is the author of more than two dozen romance novels and novellas. She is a three-time RITA® Award finalist, a four-time National Readers' Choice Awards finalist, the winner of a Rising Star Award in traditional romantic fiction and was nominated for Series Storyteller of the Year by RT Book Reviews in 2008. She makes her home in mid-Michigan with her husband and their two children. She enjoys gardening and gabbing and can be reached on Facebook at facebook.com/authorjackiebraun or through her website at **www.jackiebraun.com**

™

Greek for Beginners

Jackie Braun

First published in Great Britain 2013
by Mills & Boon, an imprint of Harlequin (UK) Limited.
Harlequin (UK) Limited, Eton House, 18-24 Paradise Road,
Richmond, Surrey TW9 1SR

© Jackie Braun Fridline 2013

ISBN: 978 0 263 23550 0

Harlequin (UK) policy is to use papers that are natural, renewable and recyclable products and made from wood grown in sustainable forests. The logging and manufacturing process conform to the legal environmental regulations of the country of origin.

Printed and bound in Great Britain
by CPI Antony Rowe, Chippenham, Wiltshire

Also by Jackie Braun

Must Like Kids
If the Ring Fits…
The Fiancée Fiasco
Confessions of a Girl-Next-Door
Mr Right There All Along
The Road Not Taken
Star-Crossed Sweethearts
Inconveniently Wed!
Sheikh in the City
Confidential: Expecting!
Boardroom Baby Surprise

Did you know these are also available as eBooks?
Visit www.millsandboon.co.uk

To Roma Costanzo
with thanks for all of her love and support!

CHAPTER ONE

IF DARCIE HAYES had any lingering doubts about her decision to call off her wedding a week before the "I dos" and end her engagement to her longtime beau, they were eradicated the moment she stepped off the plane in Athens and scanned the crowd.

A driver was supposed to meet her at the airport. That was part of the nonrefundable, all-inclusive Greek tour package that her spendthrift fiancé had booked for their honeymoon. The honeymoon she had decided to take alone.

Tad got their Buffalo, New York, condominium and their antisocial cat in the breakup. She'd figured a couple of weeks away from her well-meaning friends and family in sun-drenched Greece was a fair trade since she'd never liked the condo, and the cat had never liked her. Now, she had the sinking feeling that Tad had gotten the better end of the deal.

She saw no hand-printed sign bearing her name. Nor was anyone smiling in welcome and waving to gain her attention. For a brief moment, a handsome man on a cell phone stopped talking and their gazes met.

Her best friend Becky's last text played through Darcie's head.

Meet a man. Have a fling. Get ur sexy back.

Becky had wanted to come on the trip, but she hadn't

been able to get the time off work on such short notice. That wasn't stopping her from giving Darcie all sorts of advice on how to spend her time, including having a fling. Well, if Darcie were going to cast caution to the wind, this would be exactly the sort of man she would pick to do it with. He was so gorgeous that her mouth threatened to fall open. It settled for watering, and she was forced to swallow or she would have drooled. The crowd of departing passengers surged around him then, obstructing her view. When the travelers cleared, he was gone.

After that, the only person who made eye contact with Darcie was a portly porter who approached with a trolley as she waited for her bags at the luggage carousel. It was just her luck that only one of the designer knock-offs showed up. It was the smaller of the two—the bag in which she'd packed her "second-string" outfits, the first string being the new clothes she'd bought especially for the trip. The bag sported wheels and a retractable handle, but the handle was out and dangling uselessly to the side. As for the wheels, one had been sheared off somehow.

The porter pointed to the missing wheel and busted handle, and then pointed to the trolley. Darcie nodded. Even though the bag was only one size up from a carry-on, when she'd hefted it onto the scale at the airport in Buffalo, she'd nearly given herself a hernia. She was more than happy to have someone else do the heavy lifting now.

The porter was old enough to be her father, but nothing about the smile he gave her was paternal. After loading her bag onto a cart, he winked. Then his gaze skimmed down and he said something in Greek that, even though she didn't know what it meant, had her checking the buttons on her blouse to be sure they were fastened.

"I, um, can take it from here," Darcie said, handing him

a couple euros for a tip and then making a shooing motion with her hands.

Alone again, she heaved a frustrated sigh. So much for the part of her itinerary that read, "You will be met at the airport by a member of our friendly and efficient English-speaking staff and taken directly to one of Athens's finest hotels."

But then what her near-miss of a husband considered "sparing no expense" on the trip of a lifetime and how the majority of people would define the concept were two different things entirely. Tad had never earned a penny that he hadn't pinched mercilessly afterward. Darcie was all for getting a good deal, but more often than not, you got what you paid for. She had a bad feeling this trip was going to be a case in point. The plane ride had been her first clue, wedged as she'd been for the long, transatlantic flight into a coach seat so narrow that even a runway model would have found the dimensions unforgiving.

Darcie wasn't a runway model, nor would she ever be mistaken for one, even if at five foot eleven she had the height. She also had curves, the kind for which words such as *big-boned* and, her personal favorite, *full-figured* had been strung together. She'd long ago reconciled herself to that fact that no amount of dieting was going to result in her being considered dainty. Instead, through hard work and an amount of discipline she hadn't known she'd possessed, she'd toned her body into its best shape ever for her wedding day. She'd planned to rock the church wearing a fitted white mermaid gown, but she'd never walked down the aisle.

That had been her choice, but still…

She headed for the nearest counter, putting her back into steering the trolley, which, she discovered, had an annoying tendency to veer to the right. All the way there, she prayed that one of the two uniformed men standing behind the counter would speak enough English to understand her.

"Excuse me," she began, smiling at both. *"Yia sas."* That meant "hello" and pretty much measured the extent of her Greek.

Luckily, one of the men replied in English, "Hello. How can I assist you?"

"Someone from my tour was supposed to meet me here and take me to my hotel, but I don't see anyone. I was hoping you might know where I should wait for them."

The man nodded. "What is the name of the company?"

"It's Zeus Tours." She rifled through her purse and produced a full-color brochure and a printout of her itinerary, which she handed to him.

The mouth under his thick moustache twitched with a smile and he nodded again. "Zeus Tours. *Ne.*"

"You know of them?"

"Ne," he said again. It meant "yes," but his amused expression didn't leave her feeling relieved. Next to him, the other man had started to chuckle.

Oh, this didn't bode well, but she forged ahead. "Um, so are they here?" She gestured to the busy terminal at large.

He glanced around. "I do not see Stavros."

The other man said something in Greek that had them sharing a laugh.

"Stavros." She repeated on a nod. "Am I supposed to meet this Stavros somewhere other than here?"

"Here. There." The man shrugged. "I suggest you have a seat and make yourself comfortable." He handed the papers back to her and pointed to a nearby bank of chairs. "It could be a while."

"A while?" Her stomach dropped.

"Stavros keeps his own schedule. If he owns a watch, he never consults it."

At this the man's coworker hooted with laughter.

Darcie was tired and growing irritable. She wanted a shower, a nap and something to eat, not necessarily in that order. It wouldn't hurt to throw in a drink somewhere, either. A nice glass of chilled white wine, perhaps. Or a shot of ouzo…straight from the bottle. What she didn't want to do was spend any more of her first day in Athens in the airport as the punch line for a joke. But she worked up a smile and offered her thanks.

She was attempting to wheel the trolley away when someone tapped her on the shoulder. Darcie turned to find the gorgeous man she'd spied earlier. Her stomach took another dive, but this time for reasons that had nothing to do with disappointment.

Up close, she realized that he was taller than she was. Darcie actually had to look up. Even if she'd been wearing the highest pair of heels she owned, she only would have been on eye level. Six foot three, she figured, and every last inch of him was packaged in firm muscle beneath an untucked white linen shirt and a pair of designer jeans that fit snugly across the thigh.

His skin was tanned, his jaw subtly shadowed. His hair was nearly black and fell across brows of the exact shade. The eyes below those brows were a rich chocolate-brown and smiling even though his mouth held only the faintest curve.

"Hello," he said.

Her tongue untied long enough for her to manage a basic greeting. "Hi."

"I could not help but overhear your conversation. Maybe I can be of help," he said in gorgeously accented English.

"I hope so." It came out on a sigh and Darcie came to her senses. "What I mean is, my fi— Um, friend booked an all-inclusive vacation package with Zeus Tours. I was

promised that someone would meet me at the airport, but…"
She lifted her shoulders in a shrug.

"Ah, Zeus Tours." Like the pair at the counter, the man
apparently was acquainted with the company, but he didn't
laugh. Rather, the corners of his mouth turned down in a
frown. "May I ask why you decided to book your trip with
that particular company?"

"My, um, friend found them on the internet and got a
really good deal."

It sounded like he said, "I am sure she did." He glanced
around then. "And where is your friend?"

Tad was probably with his mother, Darcie mused. It had
taken her six years to accept the fact that an engagement
ring was no match for the tight knots in Evelyn's apron
strings.

"Couldn't make it," she replied, leaving off the telltale
pronoun.

A pair of dark brows rose. "So, you came to Greece by
yourself?"

Even a man who looked like a Greek god could be a psychopathic killer. So, Darcie said carefully, "Yes, but you
know, it's a guided tour and they're expecting me."

The man glanced around and then back at her.

"Well, I'm sure someone will be here…any minute." She
pulled out the brochure again and tapped the front of it with
the tip of one finger. "I've been assured a *safe* and *super-
vised* good time over the course of the next two weeks."

This time the man's mouth joined his eyes in smiling.

"I apologize. I am making you nervous when I am only
trying to help. Here." He pulled out the cell phone she'd
seen him talking on earlier. "If you give me the number, I
will call the company for you. I know the owner. He and I
went to grade school together."

A psychopathic killer wouldn't offer to make phone calls, she reasoned. She handed him the brochure.

Darcie could hear only one side of the conversation and it was in rapid-fire Greek, but she could figure out easily enough that the handsome stranger was irritated on her behalf. Whoever was on the other end of the line was getting an earful. When the man concluded the call, he returned the phone to his back pocket.

"Well?" she asked.

"Unfortunately, your ride has been delayed. I will take you to your hotel."

"You…but…" she sputtered and glanced around, torn. She was eager to leave the airport, unpack and unwind in the comfort of her hotel room, but… "I don't even know your name."

He smiled. "I am Nick. Nick Costas. The men at the counter can vouch for me, if you would like. I fly in and out of this airport often enough. Or I can show you some identification." Without waiting for a reply, he pulled out his wallet and produced his driver's license.

"The State of New York?" She glanced up. "You're American?"

"Yes, for the past five years, but much of my family still lives in Athens. Between business and family, I am here often." He pocketed his wallet. "And you are?"

Single now.

She cleared her throat and in a demure voice managed to respond, "Darcie Hayes of Buffalo. We're practically neighbors."

It was a stretch given that his address was on Park Avenue in Manhattan and she lived upstate, several hours away. They shared a time zone but were worlds apart based on the designer watch strapped to his wrist.

Still, he was attracted to her.

She may have been long out of practice when it came to flirting, but she knew male interest when she saw it. For a woman who'd spent several years waiting to walk down the aisle while her boyfriend deferred to his mother's wishes, it was heady stuff indeed.

"It's good to meet you, Darcie Hayes of Buffalo."

He offered a hand and their palms met briefly. The simple contact managed to make her insides quake. Of course, they were shaky to begin with as a result of exhaustion and the fact that she'd bypassed the in-flight meal of mystery meat coated in unappetizing neon yellow gravy. Still, she pulled back her hand, worried she might make a fool of herself.

"It's nice to meet you, too. And I really appreciate your help." She tucked a hank of hair behind one ear. "Um, what did the tour company people say?"

"Stavros is…indisposed."

Stavros, there was that name again. Nick said he'd gone to school with the man who owned the company, but she asked hopefully, "Is this Stavros the driver?"

"The driver, the tour guide and the owner of Zeus Tours."

"Oh, boy. A real multitasker, hmm?" She blew out a breath. "When you say indisposed, what does that mean exactly? Has he fallen and broken his leg? Or contracted a nasty virus and is racked with fever?"

Nick shook his head. "Stavros is still lying in bed. He told me that he had a late night out with his friends and overindulged."

"He's h-h-hung over?" she sputtered incredulously.

"I am afraid so."

Darcie gritted her teeth. She should have known. The moment Tad bragged that he'd gotten a great deal, it should have been abundantly clear that the dream Greek honeymoon trip he'd booked was too good to be true for a reason.

"I was really hoping this Stavros had a stomach bug,"

she muttered. This surprised a laugh out of Nick. She asked him, "How familiar are you with Zeus Tours?"

Nick wasn't laughing now. "I am familiar enough to know that Stavros pours more money down his throat than he puts back into his company. He took over when his father died two years ago. In that time, he has had to let go more than half of his employees. He is not a bad man, but neither is he a good businessman."

Although she wasn't normally one to air her complaints to a stranger, weariness had her muttering, "Terrific. Just terrific. I'm here for a vacation. God knows, I'm due for one. I haven't had a day off work in two years. I've worked overtime and taken every crappy assignment I was handed without complaint so I could save up money for…for…" She waved a hand and tried to reel in her emotions. "Anyway, I was counting on the vacation described in the brochure—first-rate accommodations, air-conditioned motor coaches for sightseeing with a knowledgeable guide, authentic Greek cuisine at some of the country's best restaurants. Is this company going to be able to deliver on *any* of its promises?"

"No." He didn't hesitate at all, making that one word all the more damning.

Darcie closed her eyes briefly. "Of course not. Half of my luggage is missing. What showed up is, well, the half I wish were missing. Not that it really matters, given that my dream vacation is turning out to be a bust and I haven't even gotten out of the airport yet." She sighed. "I should have taken the condo and Rufus."

"Rufus?"

"Also know as the spawn of Satan. He's a cat," she added when Nick continued to frown. Not that her explanation made anything clear. She shook her head. "Never mind. Trust me when I say, this is the story of my life."

"Come." Nick smiled. "You can share this story of your life on the drive to your hotel."

Why not?

Darcie decided to listen to the little voice telling her that Nick Costas wasn't a threat. After all, it was the same little voice that had told her to cut all ties and run where her ex-fiancé was concerned, so she figured it knew what it was talking about. It had taken her several years to pay attention the last time. She only had two weeks in Greece. She was going to make the most of them. Starting now.

"In the mood for a good laugh, are you?" she asked wryly.

Nick smiled again. Oh, he was in the mood…for something. A diversion at the very least, and he figured he'd found one. A pretty one, too, given the woman's tumble of chestnut hair, wide-set Aegean blue eyes and a body that would have made the ancient goddesses green with envy.

He'd come to the airport that day with every intention of leaving Greece and returning to his home in Manhattan. He'd booked a flight to New York, a flight that would be boarding shortly without him. Just as well. He'd been angry with his family and their unabashed matchmaking and had allowed his emotions to cloud his judgment.

Of course, he would have to be back in Greece within a fortnight anyway. No amount of irritation would cause him to miss his brother's wedding. He would never live down the talk otherwise. And there was plenty of that already since Pieter was marrying Nick's childhood sweetheart, Selene.

Half of Athens was gossiping about it, waiting for a fight to erupt between the brothers. Nick was determined not to indulge the gawkers, as awkward and, yes, painful, as the situation was. He lamented the strain between him and Pieter. He regretted the division in his once unified family. But neither could be helped. The best he could do was to gather up his dignity and feign indifference.

"Allow me," he told Darcie and took over pushing the trolley. Five steps later, he nearly took out a bank of unoccupied chairs.

"It wants to go in circles," she warned.

She was shaking her head and smiling. He liked her smile. Her lips were inviting even without any added gloss. A lovely diversion, he thought again.

And why not? He was entitled. He had no strings to tangle him up. He hadn't had those since Selene. That was the way he preferred it, too, as he'd pointed out to his grandmother that very morning when Yiayia expressed concern about his ongoing single status. Nick had no such concerns. What he had was a plan, a meticulously crafted five-year plan to grow his auction business. After that, he might start thinking about settling down, but never again would he allow his heart to be broken. Once was enough.

"Is this part of the story of your life?" he asked Darcie, motioning to the wayward cart.

"That's right." She lowered her voice to a confidential whisper. "I probably shouldn't tell you this, but since you're being so nice, I feel I owe you the truth. I'm a magnet for bad luck."

"Really?"

"Really. Swear." She traced a cross over her very impressive chest.

Nick followed the progress of her fingertip before allowing his gaze to lift to her lips again. "Perhaps your luck is about to change."

CHAPTER TWO

WHILE SHE WAITED for Nick to retrieve his car from the long-term parking lot, Darcie called Becky. Even if she didn't think Nick was a psycho, she decided it would be wise to let someone know she had arrived safely in Athens and was now in the hands of a stranger. Calling her parents was out of the question. Ditto for her sisters. That left Becky, who answered on the fifth ring.

"Someone had better be dying," her friend muttered ominously, and Darcie realized it was the middle of the night in Buffalo.

"I'm not dying, just checking in," she said. "Sorry I woke you, Becks. I forget about the time difference."

"Darcie? Oh. Hey." She pictured Becky struggling to a sitting position on her bed and trying to force the cobwebs from her head. "Is everything okay?"

Darcie scuffed the toe of one shoe against the pavement. "Sort of."

"What does that mean?"

"Well, my flight arrived on time, but I'm missing half of my luggage. The good half."

Becky had helped her pack, so she commiserated. "That stinks. On the bright side, now you have a valid excuse to buy more clothes."

"Yeah." Like Darcie could afford to do that. She coughed

and continued. "Oh, and there's been one other small glitch. No one from the tour company was at the airport to meet me."

"What? That's ridiculous. You need to report them to the Better Business Bureau or something."

"I know. Apparently, the owner of the company is a lush." She forced out a laugh. "Figures, right? I mean, Tad got such a good deal on this vacation there was bound to be a catch."

Becky muttered something obscene about Tad. It wasn't anything Darcie hadn't heard before. Her friend had been quite vocal in her dislike of him. That had been a source of contention between the two women in the past, but no longer. She found herself wondering what Becky would make of Nick.

"I hope the rest of the trip goes smoothly," her friend said.

Unfortunately, based on what Nick had told Darcie, she had her doubts. She told Becky as much.

"What are you going to do? Can you get a refund and hook up with a different company?"

"I don't know." The fine print on the package said the price was nonrefundable, but Darcie planned to try anyway. She figured she had nothing to lose. "In the meantime, I have a ride to the first hotel on the itinerary. The tour group is supposed to stay there for a couple of nights. That should give me time to see if the company is going to be able to deliver on any of its promises and, if not, make other arrangements." At least she hoped it would.

"Good. Darcie, if you need money—"

"No. I don't. But thanks." Not only could Becky not afford it, but she'd also been generous enough already, letting Darcie crash at her apartment until she found a place of her own. That certainly beat moving back in with her parents, even temporarily. What thirty-year-old woman wanted to do that?

Darcie took a deep breath then and, keeping her tone nonchalant, said, "You're going to love this. The person who agreed to drive me is this insanely gorgeous man with an accent that is to die for."

There was a slight pause before Becky asked, "You're taking a cab, right?"

"No. Actually, I met this man in the airport and he… offered to drive. He showed me identification," she hastened to add. "His name is Nick Costas. He lives in Manhattan, but he's from Athens originally."

"Darcie, I don't know," Becky began, worry evident in her tone.

"What happened to, 'Have a fling and get ur sexy back?' Hmm?"

"Well, I didn't actually expect you to take my advice! When do you ever listen to me? I mean, if you listened to me, you never would have given Tad the time of day, much less wasted six years of your life engaged to him."

Point taken. Becky had told Darcie from the start that Tad was a first-class mama's boy and would stay that way.

"Relax. I'm not having a fling. It's only a ride to a hotel. Nothing more." Except maybe in her fantasies.

"Okay, but call me when you get there."

"I will."

"Promise me, Darcie. I'm not going to be able to go back to sleep until you do."

"I promise. I'll call."

She hung up just as Nick's car pulled to the curb. Unlike the other boxy subcompacts parked nearby, it was a sleek, low-slung convertible.

"Nice car." She tapped a finger to her lips as she studied its graceful lines. "A 1963 Porsche, right?"

He nodded slowly. "A 356 Super 90 Cabriolet, to be exact."

"Fully restored?"

"Yes, but with original parts. And I have a certificate of authenticity from the manufacturer."

"Ooh. That pushes up its value."

"It does." Nick tilted his head to the side. "How is it that you know so much about automobiles?"

Darcie chuckled at his incredulous expression. "I work for a classic car magazine. I guess I picked up a few things along the way."

"You're a writer."

She frowned. Not for lack of wanting, she thought. "No. I just check the facts of articles other people write."

"Which magazine might that be?"

"*Automobile Enthusiasts Monthly.* It's relatively small and based in Buffalo. You probably haven't heard of it." Darcie hadn't until Tad's friend had offered her the job just before her engagement.

"I have a subscription. I find it very *factual.*" He got out of the car and stood beside her. "What else can you tell me about this particular model Porsche?"

"Well, as I recall, it was very popular in America when it first came out."

"It still is among collectors."

"And you're a collector." It made sense. A man with a Park Avenue address likely would have the disposable income to indulge his whims, even ones that ran into six figures.

But Nick was shaking his head. "I collect for others. As much as I like this automobile, I will not be buying it. It will go to whoever pays the most to possess it. It is what I do for a living." He pulled out a business card, which he handed to her. It read, Costas Classic Auto Sales and Auctions.

"Impressive."

"It would appear that you and I have two interests in common."

"Two?"

"Classic cars and…" His smile could have melted a glass and made it clear what that other interest was. She smiled in return and hoped the laughter that followed came off as worldly rather than the sort fueled by giddiness and nerves.

"Let me take your bag," he said.

The Porsche had a rear engine, meaning its trunk was in the front. When Nick opened the compartment, Darcie eyed the small space.

"Gee, maybe it's just as well the airline lost one of my bags. I don't think both of them would fit in here. I guess when you own one of these babies you have to travel light to travel in style." She glanced at Nick, a question forming. "Where's your luggage?"

The left side of his mouth rose. "On a plane bound for New York." At her puzzled expression, he added, "I was planning to fly back today."

"Why did you change your mind?"

"I decided I was being rash."

"So you missed your flight and offered assistance to a perfect stranger instead," she replied dryly. Talk about rash…and flattering. Just wait until she told Becky *that.* Her friend was going to hyperventilate. As it was, Darcie's breathing was a little uneven.

"A stranded stranger," Nick corrected. His smile was full-blown this time and very effective. "One who is also very beautiful."

Her heart fluttered and she blinked. "Oh."

"You are blushing."

"I, um…" She waved a hand, not certain how to reply.

"Surely, you have been told before that you are beautiful?"

"Of course I have." She rolled her eyes. "All the time, in fact. We're talking daily. It gets old."

The truth was no, at least not in the past several years. Tad wasn't one for compliments. Even during the courtship phase of their relationship, pretty words had been few and far between. After he'd slid an engagement ring on her finger? Forget about it.

"You know how I feel about you, Darcie. That should be enough."

Maybe it should have been. But it wasn't. Every now and then, especially when she was PMSing and feeling bloated and unattractive, a compliment would have been nice.

And then there was his mother. Evil Evelyn, as Becky had dubbed her. The older woman was quick with thinly veiled digs about Darcie's appearance, including her good "birthing hips."

"You are beautiful," Nick said again. "And your blush only makes you more so."

This time, Darcie accepted the compliment with what she hoped was a gracious smile. *Beautiful.* Why not? Wasn't beauty in the eye of the beholder? And what a beholder.

Nick opened the car door for her before heading around to the driver's side. It was another small courtesy that made her feel like she'd stepped into some sort of fairy tale.

"Shall I put up the top?"

"No," she told him. "Leave it down. I can use the fresh air after all those hours in a stuffy airplane."

And, okay, in her fairy tale, a ride in a Porsche convertible only added to the romance.

He was seated behind the wheel now. "Even if it means tangled hair?" He reached over and coiled the end of one lock around his index finger. If he wound it any tighter, she would be forced to lean closer to him.

While their gazes held, she blindly plumbed the depths of her oversized purse until her fingers encountered an elastic band. Pulling it out with the same verve a magician uses to produce a white rabbit, she announced, "I believe I have a solution for that."

Nick eyed the elastic band a moment before uncoiling the lock, and she hastily tugged her hair into a ponytail.

"Very clever, but you missed some."

This time, he made contact with more than her hair. His fingertips were warm against her cheek as they corralled the wayward strands and tucked them behind her ear. The gesture might have been construed as friendly if not for the gleam in his dark eyes or the Richter-scale-worthy effect it had on her pulse.

A car horn blasted behind them. Its driver yelled something in Greek. Nick yelled something back in the same language, but his tone was more circumspect than annoyed, and his expression could only be described as pleased.

To Darcie, he said, "People are in too much of a hurry. I prefer to take things slowly. Rushing is no good."

With that, he turned the key in the car's ignition. The Porsche's powerful engine growled to life and they were off.

Nick wasn't familiar with the hotel listed on her itinerary, but he plugged the address to The Santor into his cell phone and downloaded directions as he merged into traffic.

"It should take about forty minutes to get there," he said as they left the airport behind.

Darcie settled back in her seat, determined to take in the sights along the way. Not only was this her first time in Greece, but it was also her first trip abroad. Indeed, other than a couple of weekend jaunts to Toronto with Becky, she'd never been outside the United States. Despite the passing scenery, however, she remained almost painfully aware of the man seated next to her, and her gaze kept returning to his profile. God, he was handsome and he'd made it plain that their attraction was mutual. This might not be a fling exactly, but it was awfully damned flattering to have such a good-looking man paying attention to her.

When he turned and caught her staring, she blurted out, "Were you always so buff? I mean, a car buff. Were you always a car buff?"

"Car buff?"

"Interested in cars," she clarified, relieved that her slip of the tongue hadn't made it past the language barrier.

He nodded. "My uncle raced them for a time, and the summer I turned sixteen, I traveled with him on the European Grand Prix circuit."

"That sounds exciting."

Nick smiled in agreement. "It was. Very."

"Did you ever race?"

"I considered it at one point, but no." He shrugged. "Ultimately, I was more interested in the cars—that is to say their overall design—than how fast they could travel on a closed course. So, when I was eighteen, I bought a 1957 Porsche Speedster I found advertised in the newspaper."

"Wow. Nice first car." Hers had been her grandmother's ancient sedan. It was the size of a small country and guzzled fuel like a college student guzzles coffee while studying for final exams. Darcie had happily traded up to the decade-old compact she still owned.

Nick was chuckling. "Not really. It needed a lot of work, which is why I could afford it. I spent the entire summer tracking down all of the parts to rebuild its engine." His smile was both nostalgic and proud.

"And you were hooked," she guessed.

She'd felt that way the first time she'd composed an article for her high school's newspaper. Three paragraphs on changes to the lunch menu and she'd known what she wanted to be when she grew up. Now, eight years after earning a degree in journalism, she could barely claim to be a journalist.

Nick was saying, "Hooked. Yes, I was. Especially after I decided to sell the Speedster at auction in Kalamai two summers later. Collectors came not only from all over Greece, but from other parts of Europe to bid on it. I loved the excitement. So, I used the money from the sale to buy another car, fix it up and auction it off. Later, I decided I did not want to go to the auctions, I wanted to run them. So, that is what I do."

She heard satisfaction in his tone. Pride. How long had it been since she'd felt either of those emotions when it came to her own job? How long had it been since she'd dreamed of bigger and better things for herself when it came to her career? Her life? Settling. Darcie had done so damned much of it.

"Did you come to Greece on business then?" she asked.

Nick shook his head and some of his dark hair fell across his forehead. It lent an air of recklessness to his already pulse-pounding good looks.

"Not this time. I came for a family wedding."

Wedding. Even spoken with Nick's gorgeous accent, the word brought Darcie up short, reminding her as it did of her recent close call with "I do." How different her life might be right now if a week ago she hadn't finally found the courage to act on what her heart—and, well, Becky—had been telling her for so long. Tad wasn't the right man for her.

"Yet you were going to leave today."

"I would have been back. The ceremony does not take place until the Saturday after next."

His response had her blinking in surprise. "That's more than two weeks away, and you're already here?"

"It is expected," he replied.

Darcie detected a slight edge to his tone and thought she understood its source. She knew all about family expectations. She had three sisters, two older, one younger, all of them happily married and busily procreating as if the survival of the human race depended on them. Meanwhile, Darcie had passed the big three-oh mark in the spring and the only thing that remained of her eagerly anticipated nuptials was the stack of gifts that would have to be returned when she got back.

A groan escaped. At Nick's quizzical glance, she said, "I feel your pain. My family can be, well, difficult to please at times. So, who's getting married?"

"My brother Pieter."

"I take it he lives here."

"Yes. As does my entire family."

Yet Nick made his home in a city across the Atlantic. Interesting. "No apron strings for you," she murmured.

"Apron strings?"

"Nothing. Are you and your brother close?"

"We used to be closer."

At that, his lips flattened into a grim line, leaving her with the distinct impression there was much more to the story. Still, she kept her curiosity in check and changed the subject. They engaged in polite small talk until they arrived at their destination. Even before she saw the hotel, she knew it would be a dive. The oath that slipped from Nick's lips told her as much.

Luxury accommodations? Right. The squat, two-story building looked like it should have a date with a wrecking ball, despite the sign out front printed in Greek and English that announced it was Under Renovation. It was more rickety than some of the country's ancient ruins. Glancing around, Darcie realized The Santor wasn't located in the best of neighborhoods, either. As hungry as she was, she didn't think she would be comfortable hoofing up the block to the restaurant she spied there. At the moment, two men were loitering out front, smoking cigarettes and passing a liquor bottle back and forth.

With her earlier hysteria threatening to return, she muttered, "Rufus really wasn't so bad."

Nick's brows drew together. "Your cat?"

"No longer. I was thinking good riddance after what he did to my favorite silk dress. But now…" She shrugged.

"Has anyone ever told you that the story of your life is very confusing?"

"Only all the time."

"I'll walk you in and see you settled."

No protest passed Darcie lips. Since it would have been token at best, she didn't see the point. No way did she want to go inside that death trap by herself.

"Thanks. I'd appreciate it."

Nick retrieved her sorry-looking bag and they made their way to the entrance on a makeshift walkway of cardboard that had been placed over mud puddles. On either side of the door were potted palm trees whose fronds were coated with thick, grayish construction dust.

Nick held open one of the grimy glass doors. "After you."

"Gee, thanks."

She took a halting step inside and waited for her eyes to adjust to the dim lighting. Once they did, she wished they hadn't. The lobby was filled with an assortment of power tools and building supplies, and every last inch of the place was as dust-coated as the palms outside. Her apprehension kicked into high gear as she imagined the condition the rooms would be in.

As if sensing her hesitation, Nick placed a hand on the small of her back and propelled her toward the reception desk. A woman stood behind it. Darcie pegged her to be about forty-five and a chain smoker. A lit cigarette dangled from her lips and a second one burned merrily in the ashtray on the countertop. The woman squinted at them through the haze created by both dust and smoke.

"Good afternoon." The greeting was offered in Greek as she set the cigarette in the ashtray.

"Good afternoon," Nick replied. His gaze flicked to her name badge and he added, "Pesha. How are you today?"

He said this in English, which Pesha apparently understood and could speak, because she switched to English as well.

"I am much better now." Her smile was flirtatious and made it clear why. Darcie couldn't fault the woman for that. Nick had certainly brightened her day. "How can I help you?"

"My friend has a reservation."

"Friend." Her smile widened and she exhaled. Residual wisps of smoke curled out from the woman's nostrils. Not terribly attractive, but they did distract one from the tar stains on her teeth. "What is the name?"

"Darcie Hayes," Nick said.

There was no computer to consult, only a thick, leather-bound book through which Pesha began flipping. Finally, she glanced up.

"Sorry. I have no one by that name registered here this week."

"Um, what about for a Darcie Franklin." It would have been her married name. She avoided meeting Nick's questioning gaze.

More page flipping ensued before Pesha shook her head. "*Oxi.* I cannot find that name among my guests, either."

"There must be some mistake. The tour package was booked months ago and paid in full."

"Tour package?" Pesha said slowly. "Which tour package might that be?"

"A multicity, sightseeing excursion that was booked through Zeus Tours."

"Stavros!"

The woman spat out the name with enough force to turn the two benign syllables into the vilest of curses. But she wasn't done. She continued in Greek, gesturing wildly the entire time. Darcie was left with no choice but to grit her teeth and listen. By the time Pesha switched to English again, she had worked up a good head of steam.

"That man owes me for the last three tour groups that stayed here. I have told him, no more! I have been turning his customers away all day."

She selected one of the cigarettes from the ashtray and took a long, lung-blackening drag.

"Um, when you say no more," Darcie began.

"I will not honor any more of his bookings unless he pays me in advance." Pesha stamped out the cigarette for emphasis.

"I can understand your annoyance with Stavros." Darcie was pretty annoyed with the man herself. "But I paid in full for a room at The Santor."

Sure, the accommodations were crap, but it was the principle of the matter. They were crap for which Tad's credit card already had been hit.

Pesha picked up the second cigarette and inhaled deeply before blowing out a stream of smoke that shot past Darcie's left shoulder. Even so, wisps of it lingered and stung her nose.

"No, you paid Stavros in full, but he has not paid me. He has not paid me for too long!" Pesha chopped at the air with the hand holding the cigarette, sending ashes flying. Darcie was only glad the woman wasn't clutching a sharp object. "And until he does, I will not be putting up any more of his tour customers. Now, if you wish to pay with cash, I will be happy to give you a room."

Darcie could see the woman's point. Pesha had a business to run and Stavros had stiffed her more than once. Still, it left Darcie in a bind, and if she had to shell out more money for a room, it sure as hell wasn't going to be in this fleabag establishment. She turned to Nick, who apparently read her mind.

"I will take you to another hotel. Perhaps something that is closer to shopping, restaurants and nightlife."

Darcie cleared her throat and added, "But reasonably priced. My budget is limited."

Pesha bristled as they turned to leave.

"You will not find a better bargain than The Santor," she insisted.

Since so much of Darcie's life was left to fate at the moment, it was with a sense of destiny that she replied, "I'll take my chances."

Mindful of what Darcie had said about her budget, Nick took her to one of the chain hotels in the city, even though it offered neither the charm nor the ambience of the nicer and pricier establishments he would have preferred. But it was conveniently located and tidy, with a smoke-free lobby and a concierge who appeared eager to please.

After she booked a room, they lingered near the bank of elevators. He wasn't in a hurry to leave. In fact, he almost regretted having to say goodbye. Darcie didn't seem eager to end their association, either.

"How good are the chances that Stavros will refund the money for my trip?" she asked.

"Not good. My guess is he does not have the money to refund."

She made a humming sound. "That's what I was afraid of. At this rate, I will be on a flight back to New York before the end of the week."

Her budget, Nick assumed. He meant it when he said, "That would be a shame. Greece is a beautiful country with so much to see."

It might not have any effect, but he planned to call Stavros on her behalf and apply a little pressure. Darcie Hayes and unsuspecting travelers like her shouldn't have to pay for the man's bad business decisions and personal habits.

Nick's reasons, of course, weren't all pure. His gaze took in the long line of her legs. Even in flat shoes she was a tall woman. *Statuesque* was the word that came to mind. Sexy applied, too, given her well-rounded curves and the toned backside he'd glimpsed. Why did he get the feeling she was unaware of the power of her allure? In his experience, most women who looked like she did weren't. They flaunted their looks, used them to get what they wanted. The fact that Darcie didn't made her not only refreshing, but also a puzzle.

Nick liked puzzles. They ranked right up there with games of chance when it came to guilty pleasures.

"I can't thank you enough for all you've done," she was saying.

"I have done nothing."

"I disagree. You've acted as my personal driver for the past couple of hours. I'd probably still be sitting in the airport with my busted-up luggage waiting for a ride that wasn't coming if it weren't for you."

She was all but tipping over on her nose. The signs of exhaustion were unmistakable, from the shadows under her eyes to the droop in her shoulders. He doubted that she would last an hour in her room before sleep claimed her, and knew a moment of regret that he wouldn't be there when she awoke.

"I am happy I could help. I would hate for a visitor to my homeland to go away with an unfavorable impression of Greek hospitality. Stavros Pappanolos's poor example notwithstanding, you will find that the people here are very generous and helpful."

"Oh, you've more than made up for Stavros."

She cleared her throat. There was that becoming blush again. Nick leaned forward, drawn by her reserve. Before he could kiss her, she held out a hand that poked into his solar plexus. Her cheeks flamed bright red now.

"Well, I guess this is where we say goodbye," she said.

Was it? Nick didn't think so. But she was tired and he had fences to mend with his family.

He took her hand and meant it when he said, "It has been entirely my pleasure, Darcie Hayes."

CHAPTER THREE

DARCIE WAS STILL on Nick's mind the following day as he sat in his grandmother's kitchen having a midmorning snack of freshly baked *koulourakia portokaliou*. The sweet, orange-flavored cookies were a staple in Yiayia's house, precisely because they ensured company.

His parents were there as well. George and Thea Costas lived right next door. In fact, Nick's entire extended family was clustered together in a small geographic area on the western edge of Athens. True to tradition, Pieter already owned a house just down the road. In two short weeks, he and Selene would live in it together as husband and wife.

Even the sweetness of the cookie wasn't enough to wipe out the bitter taste in Nick's mouth.

"Your tea is growing cold," Yiayia said, interrupting his thoughts. The snow-white hair coiled on her head made a striking contrast to her usual black frock. Sophia Pappas had been a widow for twenty-three years and still wore the color of mourning. She also considered it her duty as the family's matriarch to meddle as she saw fit. "And you are frowning, Nikolos. Is something wrong with my cookies?"

"Nothing is wrong with your cookies." He took another bite and smacked his lips for emphasis. "I just have a lot on my mind."

"This is a difficult time for you." His grandmother nodded sagely.

"Only because everyone insists on making it so."

"Have you given any more thought to Pieter's request?" his mother asked.

It took an effort not the crush the cookie that remained in his hand. Pieter wanted Nick to be his *koumbaro* or best man at the upcoming Greek Orthodox ceremony. As such, it would be Nick who put the crowns on Pieter and Selene's heads and switched them back and forth three times to symbolize their union.

Nick wanted no part of that. He couldn't believe his brother even had the nerve to ask.

"I have said no too many times to count, Mama."

She frowned. "I wish you would reconsider. He is your brother, Nick. Your *only* brother."

"Pieter conveniently forgot that when he started seeing Selene behind my back."

"You were gone, Nick. You went to America to start your business," Thea reminded him unnecessarily. "You told Selene you understood when she said she did not want to move to New York, too."

What Nick understood was betrayal. Despite what he'd told Selene at the time, he'd held out hope that she would change her mind. In his heart, he'd believed that the two of them would marry eventually. Until Pieter.

"I will not be his *koumbaro*. Be happy that I have agreed to attend the wedding at all."

"Be happy, be happy," Yiayia chided with a shake of her head. "You would do well to listen to your own advice, my boy. You will not find a bride of your own if you do not look."

"I can assure you, I do not lack for female companionship."

"Take care how you speak around your grandmother," George interjected gruffly.

Nick recognized the tone. It was the same one his father had used when Nick stepped over the line as a boy. He was over the line now, too. And so he apologized.

"I am merely trying to point out that if I wanted a wife I would have one."

He wouldn't call himself the black sheep of the family, but his wool was definitely dyed a different shade than his brother's, much to his mother's and Yiayia's regret. In addition to his Manhattan apartment, Nick kept a house just outside Athens near the Aegean. His whitewashed home was situated on a hillside and boasted panoramic views of a harbor that was dotted with yachts and fishing boats. His mother claimed the view soothed his restless nature. In some ways, watching all of those boats sail out into open waters only fed it.

"The women you know in Manhattan are not proper wife material," his mother said.

This was true enough, in part because at this point in his life, with a business to build and the related travel taking up so much of his time, he wasn't ready to settle down.

Still, he couldn't resist asking, "How do you know this, Mama? You have not met any of the women I have been with since Selene."

"I do not need to meet them. I am your mother. I know." Thea folded her arms.

He loved his family. He loved Greece. But ever since he'd sold that first automobile to a collector living in the United States more than a decade earlier, he'd known that he would never settle for the quiet and predictable life he would have endured living here and working with his father.

His family had never understood Nick's obsession with classic cars and his desire to see them restored, much less the pleasure he took from connecting a collector with exactly what he or she sought. They were proud of him, certainly. Through hard work, shrewd investment and a little bit of luck, Nick had managed to turn his passion into a multimillion-dollar enterprise. They just wished he'd decided to base it in Athens rather than New York.

"Besides, those women are not Greek," Yiayia said.

It boiled down to that for his grandmother. His mother, too, though she was less inclined to say so out loud. Both women wanted Nick to marry a nice Greek girl, preferably one from a family they knew, so that he would return home, buy a house nearby and settle in. It wasn't going to happen, but that didn't keep them from trying.

Sure enough, his mother was saying, "I saw Maria Karapoulos at the market yesterday. Her daughter Danika was with her. She has moved back from London. Her job there didn't work out."

"Just as well. They don't know how to make a proper cup of tea in England," Yiayia observed. Both women laughed. "How does Danika look? As pretty as ever?"

"Prettier," Thea said. "She has lost some weight, and I think she has contacts now. She wasn't wearing her glasses. She has such lovely eyes."

"And she comes from a nice family," his grandmother noted.

Nick sipped his tea and said nothing. The eyes he was thinking about were blue and belonged to Darcie.

His mother went on. "I invited her to the wedding. Her parents were already on the guest list. It seemed rude not to extend an invitation to her as well."

"Good. Good. She will have fun at the wedding," Yiayia said. "Especially if she has someone to dance with."

Even though his tea was plenty sweet, Nick added a little

more honey and tried to ignore the conversation going on around him. But he knew what was coming.

Sure enough, his grandmother added, "Nick could be her escort."

He gave his tea a vigorous stir. "No."

How many times must they go through this particular exercise before his mother and grandmother accepted that he didn't need or want their help to find a date? He'd considered asking one of the local women to come with him just to get Thea and Yiayia off his back, but that posed a problem of its own. Thanks to all of the gossip, the single women in his social circle saw Nick as a challenge or as an object of pity. He didn't want to be viewed as either.

He glanced over at his father, hoping for an ally, but George pushed his chair away from the table and rose. Motioning over his shoulder, he said, "The drain in the bathroom sink is running slow. I promised your grandmother I would take a look at it."

"I will give you a hand," Nick offered.

But George shook his head. "No. You finish your tea. I can manage on my own."

"Thank you, Papa," Nick drawled sarcastically.

His father stopped at the doorway. "You might listen to your mother, you know. I remember this Danika she speaks of. The girl comes from a good family. You could do worse."

Now there was a recommendation. The room was quiet after his father's exit. Nick was just starting to think the topic had been dropped when his mom said, "You are not going with anyone. It would be a shame for two young, single people to attend alone."

Yiayia clapped her hands together. "So it is settled. Nikolos will take her."

"No. I will not take her."

"No?"

Nick blotted his mouth with a napkin and worked to keep his tone civil. "I am not going to take Danika or any of the other women you two have suggested to the wedding. I have said no and I mean no."

"No! No! Always no!" His grandmother gestured with her arms before demanding, "Give us one good reason why not."

A curvy young woman with deep blue eyes, killer legs and a thick, wavy mane of hair came to mind and inspiration struck.

"I have a date."

Both older women blinked in surprise. His mother was the first to find her voice. "You have a date?" she asked skeptically.

"For the wedding?" Yiayia added, her tone equally dubious.

Lying did not come easily to Nick, no matter how good he considered the cause, so he answered her question with one of his own. "Is that so hard to believe? I am not repulsive, you know."

"You are as handsome as Adonis," his mother affirmed, undeterred. "But just yesterday you stormed out of here after the grocer's daughter happened by and your *yiayia* invited her in for a cup of tea."

"Happened by?" His brows rose. "She was dressed for cocktails, not tea. It was a setup. I do not appreciate your matchmaking. Nor do I need your help, as well-intentioned as it may be."

Thea sighed. Nick hoped that was a sign that the matter would be dropped, at least for now. Unfortunately, his grandmother wasn't done.

"Who is this woman you have invited to your brother's wedding? When did this happen? You have not mentioned her before."

Since nothing had actually happened yet and very well might never, Nick decided to answer Yiayia's other question first. "You do not know her. She is an American."

"American." His grandmother put a hand to her chest and frowned.

"It is not a disease, you know." He chuckled, hoping both to lighten the mood and to divert the conversation. Neither woman cracked a smile, however.

"You know her from New York?" Thea asked.

"Actually, I met Darcie in Greece." Which wasn't a lie. He saw no need to mention when or where.

"Darcie. What kind of a name is Darcie?" Yiayia's frown deepened. "It does not sound like a Greek name."

His mother had other concerns. "Does she live in Athens?"

"No. She came here on holiday."

When his conscience bucked, he rationalized that he wasn't lying to his mother and grandmother. He was merely offering a selective version of the truth.

"What does she do for a living?" Yiayia inquired.

"She works at a car magazine." Beyond that, Nick knew precious little about Darcie Hayes other than the fact that he found her very attractive. At the moment, he also found her his ticket out of a tight spot. "I tell you what. I will bring her by some time and you can ask her all of these questions yourselves."

He thought he was off the hook, or at the very least had delayed his day of reckoning. Yiayia dispelled that notion.

"Good. I will set an extra plate for supper."

"S-supper?" he sputtered. "Tonight?"

"We will eat at seven."

"Come early," his mother added with an eager smile that sent his insides churning.

What had he gotten himself into?

* * *

Darcie had forced herself to stay awake until 9:00 p.m. the previous evening. She'd called Becky as promised and explained about her changed itinerary, after which she had collapsed face-first on the bed and slept like the dead. When she awoke just before ten o'clock the following morning she had a deep crease from the sheets across her right cheek, but after nearly thirteen hours of uninterrupted slumber she felt almost human. She also was starving again.

If the tour had panned out as advertised, she already would have enjoyed a buffet breakfast with her fellow travelers and been boarding an air-conditioned motor coach headed for the Parthenon on the Acropolis. She showered and dressed, donning tan shorts and a fitted white T-shirt before lacing up a pair of sneakers. For one moment she allowed herself to picture the floral sundress and new sandals in her missing luggage. Shaking off her wistfulness, she headed for the door, eager to leave the hotel and start exploring. The day before, she'd been too exhausted to do more than walk up the block from the hotel to a small market that the concierge had recommended. She'd bought bread and fresh fruit. Today, she was in the mood for a real meal and ancient ruins.

It came as a total surprise when the first sight to greet her when she entered the lobby was Nick Costas striding purposefully through the main door. He broke into a smile that made her knees weak. It buoyed her ego that he appeared so pleased to see her.

"Darcie. Excellent. You are still here."

"Hello, Nick. Is something wrong?"

"Wrong?" He shook his head. "Not at all."

She narrowed her eyes. "Why do I sense a *but* coming?"

"Because you are too perceptive." He laughed. "You were on your way out."

"Yes. To eat."

"May I join you?"

"Okay. I should warn you that I'm not sure exactly where I'm going. I was just planning to wander around until I found a restaurant that looked appealing."

"May I make a suggestion then?"

"By all means."

"I know a wonderful spot not far from here that makes the best moussaka."

"Moussaka. My favorite," she said, although she had no idea what it was. Intrigued by both the meal and the man, Darcie agreed.

Nick took her to an out-of-the-way café that made her feel as if she had stepped back in time thanks to the building's neoclassical architecture. Conversations stopped as they wound their way to a table in the back of the small, crowded establishment. Darcie got the feeling she was the only tourist among the patrons. After giving her a cursory glance, however, the other guests returned their attention to their own tables.

A waiter appeared not long after they settled in their seats and took their order. She asked for the moussaka, in part because Nick had recommended it, and because she was unfamiliar with the other items on the menu. He ordered the same, as well as coffee for the pair of them and a bottle of sparkling water.

"I get the feeling I'm in store for an authentic Greek meal," she said once they were alone.

"You are. I hope you like it."

Her stomach was growling loud enough to be embarrassing. "I'm sure I will," she told him. "Um, what exactly is moussaka?"

His rich laughter rumbled. The sound was pleasing, especially since she didn't feel his amusement came at her expense.

"It is a dish made with eggplant. Do you like eggplant?" he asked.

"I love it. Yum."

She'd eaten it…once. It had been breaded and pan-fried, and then slathered in Evelyn's homemade tomato sauce and melted parmesan cheese. The indigestion Darcie had experienced afterward likely had been the result of Tad's mother's fault-finding throughout the meal rather than the food itself.

Nick apparently wasn't fooled. "You are an adventurous one, I see. Willing to try new things."

She liked his assessment, even if the speculative gleam in his eye gave her pause.

"I believe in being open-minded. Why not take a few chances?"

Nick smiled. "Why not indeed?"

A moment of silence passed as he studied her. She found it hard not to fidget given the intensity of his gaze. Was he picturing her naked? Darcie sucked in her stomach just to be on the safe side and found the courage to ask, "Perhaps you should tell me what's on your mind."

"A favor."

"Oh." She stopped holding in her stomach.

"You look disappointed?"

She brushed her hair back from her face. "Not at all. Ask away. Ask for anything. I owe you."

This time his laughter was low, intimate and ridiculously arousing. "That is not the sort of thing you should tell a man, *agapi mou*. If I were without scruples, you could find yourself in trouble after making a statement such as that."

Darcie was too intrigued and too attracted to Nick to be alarmed. Maybe it was the warmth that radiated from his dark eyes, or the slightly self-deprecating quirk of his sensual lips. She was sure he posed no threat to her safety. To her sanity? Well, that remained to be seen.

"But you do have scruples."

"How can you tell?"

"A man without them would not have bothered to help me yesterday without asking for anything in return."

"Yet here I am one day later, begging a favor." His lips quirked again.

"Begging is different than demanding. A man without scruples would demand, I think."

"I am glad you see it that way." His expression sobered then. "You are certainly under no obligation to agree to my proposition. I want to make that perfectly clear from the outset."

Proposition? The mere word, said as it was in that delicious accent, caused heat to curl low in Darcie's belly. Sitting with Nick inside the little café, she felt worldly, sophisticated and a lifetime removed from the awkward young woman from Buffalo who had allowed herself to be browbeaten into inertia by Tad's overbearing mother.

Darcie was pleased to find her voice was magnificently matter-of-fact when she replied, "It's clear, Nick. So, what is this proposition of yours?"

"I would like to invite you to dinner tonight."

"Dinner?" She blinked.

Maybe she'd heard him wrong. Darcie wasn't disappointed, but she was somewhat surprised. Sharing another meal seemed, well, a little mundane given his dramatic lead-in. Maybe *proposition* had a different meaning in Greece than it did back in the United States. Or maybe she'd imagined the speculative gleam in his eyes. Or maybe she was just too long out of practice with members of the opposite sex to be able to figure out their intentions beyond mere flirting.

"Dinner. Yes." He hesitated then before adding. "With my family."

Her mouth fell open at that. She knew she was gaping, yet it was a full thirty seconds before she could force her lips to close. She'd dated Tad for more than a year before he'd taken her home to meet his mother. Little had she known then that he'd been doing her a favor. Still...

"Are you going to say anything?" Nick asked at last. A grin lurked around the corners of his mouth.

"Sorry," she mumbled. "I'm just a little surprised by the invitation."

"I have no doubt of that. We have only just met, after all. And it is a big favor to ask."

The server returned with their bottle of water, a couple of glasses and two demitasse cups of coffee, forestalling her reply. Darcie took a sip of the coffee. It was stronger than she was used to, very sweet and hot enough that it burned her tongue. She barely noticed the pain. She was too preoccupied with the gorgeous man sitting across from her. Things like this didn't happen to her. There had to be a catch. Or a camera crew lurking nearby, waiting to jump out and tell her she'd been punked.

She glanced around, ruled out a hoax and asked, "Why do you want me to meet your parents?"

"Not only my parents. My grandmother will be there as well."

"Why not?" She lifted her shoulders. "The more the merrier."

"Yes." But there was nothing merry about his expression. He looked downright grim.

"So, um, why? Not that I'm not flattered by the invitation," she hastened to assure him. "But I'm curious."

"I told you that I was in Athens because my brother is to be married."

She nodded. "In two weeks."

"My mother and grandmother have had their heads together for months trying to find a date for me."

"You can't find one on your own?" Darcie winced as soon as the words were out. "What I mean is, so you are single." She winced again and picked up her coffee, braving a second burn on her tongue if it would keep her from blurting out any more embarrassing remarks.

"I'm not in a relationship at the moment." A pair of dark brows rose. "And you? I should have thought to ask if you are involved with anyone."

"Nope. No one."

And she had to admit, her emancipation—that was how she was coming to view it—felt pretty darned good right now. She was free. Free of Tad's lukewarm affection and his mother's passive-aggressive jabs. Free of her own mother's well-meaning interference and her married sisters' well-meaning advice. Free of self-doubt. Well, mostly free. Yes, Darcie was happily free to flirt, to enjoy the company of a handsome man and to accept, if she so chose, his invitation to dinner.

And she so chose.

His dark eyes warmed. "That is good. Very good."

"Oh?"

"It would not do for me to be propositioning a woman who is already spoken for."

"No worries there." Feeling emboldened, she added, "I speak for myself these days."

"Another reason to like you. Now, back to my predicament. My mother and grandmother mean well. They think I am pining."

"Pining?" She didn't like the sound of that. It implied another woman was in the picture.

He shook his head. "Perhaps lonely is a better word."

Better, but improbable. "I don't think so. You don't look lonely to me."

More to the point, men who looked *like* Nick Costas didn't tend to get lonely. They tended to have smartphones filled with the names and numbers of women who were eager to share meals and mattress space.

Nick took a sip of his coffee. "Lacking for companionship," he said at last.

Laughter bubbled out before she could stop it. "Sorry. I find that even harder to believe."

"Unfortunately, my mother and grandmother are less inclined to see the truth. So, they have been...matchmaking. I told them I have no need for their help."

"Because you can get your own dates."

"Yes, as our lunch proves. But..." The corners of his mouth turned down and he shrugged.

"How do I figure into this?"

Darcie thought she knew, and she was already flattered, but since jumping to conclusions was her specialty, she decided a little clarification wouldn't hurt. Besides, it would be really embarrassing if she was wrong.

"There is a woman who recently returned to Greece after living in London for a few years. My mother knows her mother, and has invited both of them to my brother's wedding. Now I am expected to be her escort. I told her and my grandmother that I already have a date. You."

The smile he sent Darcie could have melted a glacier. She shivered anyway and gooseflesh pricked her arms.

"Oh." Her mouth threatened to fall open again. She kept it closed by putting her elbow on the tabletop and propping her chin on her fist.

"What is this look?" he asked, his eyes narrowing as he studied her face.

She dropped the hand from her chin and busied herself

lining up the cutlery next to her plate. "I was going for non-chalant, but I suppose you could call it gobsmacked."

"Gobsmacked? I am not familiar with this term."

"Um, it means shocked."

"Because we barely know one another," he guessed.

"Sure." She moved the knife one-sixteenth of an inch to the right. "That reason will do."

"It is a lot to ask, but I was hoping you would agree." When she continued to fuss with her utensils, he reached across the table and settled his hand over hers. "I would be most grateful."

Darcie glanced up and moistened her lips. It was all Nick could do not to moan. That sexy mouth of hers was going to be his undoing. The table was narrow enough that it would take little effort to lean across it and kiss her. It was tempting. *She* was tempting.

"I don't speak Greek," Darcie said, interrupting his fantasy.

For a moment, he wasn't sure he could speak at all.

"Nick?"

He cleared his throat, bemused by the strange infatuation he felt. "That will not be a problem. Both of my parents are fluent in English, and my grandmother knows enough to get by. I can always translate if she does not understand something or if you do not."

"That's…good."

And still she hesitated. So, he decided to sweeten the deal. "Have you had any luck getting a refund on your tour?"

"No. I left a message last night and planned to call again today."

Nick had left messages as well. Stavros was either passed out cold or screening his calls. If Nick had to bet on one, he would put money on the former.

"What if I were to be your guide? In return for accompanying me to dinner, I will take you to the sites mentioned on the tour's brochure."

And why not? It would give him something to do for the next couple of weeks while he dodged his mother and grandmother's well-meaning mediation and Pieter's ongoing attempts to bury the hatchet. And he couldn't think of another woman he'd rather pass the time with than Darcie.

"That's very generous of you, but without a refund from Stavros I can't afford to stay in Greece much longer, let alone for the full two weeks."

"Leave Stavros to me."

One way or another, Nick would see to it that Darcie Hayes had her trip…and enjoyed it.

"You do realize I will be heading home the day before your brother gets married, right?"

"That is fine."

Nick did not need an actual date for Pieter's wedding. All he needed was a viable reason in the interim to avoid a setup. Once his mother and grandmother met Darcie, they would cease and desist in their matchmaking. As solutions went, it was perfect. Now if only his family would stop trying to force a reconciliation between him and Pieter.

"I don't know," Darcie began. "It sounds as if I'm getting the better end of the deal."

She only thought so because she hadn't yet met his *yiayia* or the rest of his kin, Nick thought wryly.

"Does that mean we *have* a deal?"

"I… Why not? Sure." She stuck out her hand just as she had the previous day.

Nick studied the long, unadorned fingers for a moment before giving in to his previous impulse. Bypassing her palm, he leaned over to kiss her full on the mouth. Her sweetness had him lingering and wishing for privacy. Unfortunately, there was none of that here. Sure enough, when he drew back, the restaurant erupted in applause and shouts of *"Opa!"*

Darcie's blush was becoming, if at odds with the frank interest evident in her eyes. Maybe she had gotten the better end of the deal after all. Not that Nick minded one bit.

Back at her hotel, Nick insisted on parking his car and walking her inside. Darcie thought she knew why. He wanted to kiss her again. Well, no problem. She wanted to kiss him again, too.

The lip-lock they'd shared in the restaurant had been amazing. On a scale of one to ten, Darcie would rate it a ten...thousand. That didn't even take into account the degree of difficulty involved. Nick had managed that score with a table wedged between them and a wide-eyed crowd of spectators, whose spontaneous applause afterward, by the way, had been entirely appropriate. Heck, that kiss had deserved a standing ovation. Darcie would settle for an encore.

Should she ask him to come up to her room? They would have privacy but it might seem too forward. He might think she wanted to sleep with him. Did she?

Why yes, she did. She was human and breathing and he was gorgeous and sexy beyond belief. But should she?

Probably not a good idea. She'd never been the sort of woman who slept with a man on the first date. Or the second. Or the third...

"Darcie—"

"Even the fourth would be pushing it."

Nick's brow wrinkled. "Excuse me?"

"Nothing." She waved a hand. "Just, um...here we are."

They had reached the elevator and Darcie still wasn't sure what she should do. He took the decision out of her hands by pushing the button.

"Are you coming up?" she asked casually.

"I would like to, but…" He shook his head.

"A gentleman," she mused.

It sounded like he said, "A fool."

"So, I'll see you to—"

He pulled her into his arms and kissed her with all of the passion and skill he'd shown in the restaurant, but with far less of the restraint.

"—night."

Nick's breath was sawing in and out, but he managed to mutter something in Greek that told Darcie he was every bit as turned on as she was.

Before the elevator arrived, he turned and walked away.

CHAPTER FOUR

DARCIE NEEDED AN outfit for dinner since nothing in her luggage full of second-string clothes seemed appropriate. But what did one wear to meet a man's parents when one barely knew the man?

She mulled that question as she wandered the labyrinth of streets near her hotel. Shops abounded, interspersed with cafés and taverns. The only problem was that the goods the stores sold were geared toward tourists: snow globes featuring miniature Parthenons, key chains and postcards. As for clothing, it fell into two categories: logoed T-shirts and the traditional Greek garb that she doubted anyone in Greece actually wore.

Two hours into her quest the arches of her feet were beginning to ache, but she decided to stray a little farther from the beaten path. After another half an hour, her persistence was rewarded when she arrived at the door of a small boutique that the owner of a nearby bakery had recommended. After licking the last crumbs of freshly made baklava from her fingertips, Darcie headed inside.

The boutique was small and totally kitsch-free. It also was expensive, with prices that reflected the quality of the garments on display. Darcie swallowed hard after glancing at the tag that dangled from a cap-sleeved cocktail dress made of red silk. She calculated the exchange rate in her head. It was far more than she felt comfortable spending, even though the dress was gorgeous. She moved on to another rack, but it was of no use. The garments there, while also lovely, were equally expensive. On a sigh, she turned to leave.

"May I help you find something?" a woman asked in English as she stepped out from behind the counter. She was about Darcie's age and nearly her height in a pair of killer high heels. The name tag pinned to her chest read Nerina.

Darcie shook her head. "I was just looking."

"For anything in particular?"

She started to say no only to admit, "I've been invited to dinner this evening."

The woman smiled knowingly. "With a man."

"Yes. He's taking me to meet his parents."

"Oh, this is serious. He is Greek?"

"No and yes." At the saleswoman's perplexed expression, Darcie added, "No, it's not serious. At least not how you mean. We've only just met and…it's not serious. But, yes, he is Greek. Well, I guess he's actually American now, but he's from Athens. Originally. You know, he was born here." She grimaced. "I'm probably not making any sense."

"I understand. You are nervous." Again, Nerina's knowing smile made an appearance. "Even though you have only just met, you like this man."

"I do."

It was the truth. What was not to like about a man who had been gracious and kind and treated her with respect, all while making it clear that he found her attractive and wouldn't mind seeing her naked?

Okay, so maybe Darcie had extrapolated that last part, but the kiss Nick had given her in the restaurant had made her toes want to curl. And the one in the lobby of her hotel?

She was surprised she hadn't spontaneously combusted in the elevator afterward.

"Then we must find you something perfect for this evening." Nerina turned to another rack and began flipping through the garments.

Darcie cleared her throat. "I'm afraid I'm on a limited budget. Actually, a very limited budget. I shouldn't be buying clothes at all, but the airline lost my luggage and…"

"And then you met this handsome man who has invited you to dinner to meet his parents, and you want to look stunning."

Darcie sighed. "That about sums it up." Placing a hand on her stomach to quell her nerves, she asked, "Do you take credit cards?"

Nerina nodded and then tapped her lips thoughtfully for a moment before bursting into a satisfied grin.

"I have just the dress."

Later that afternoon, freshly showered, Darcie took her time getting ready, shimmying first into a bra and panties that weren't likely to be seen, but made her feel sexy and sophisticated nonetheless. Both pieces were lacy and utterly feminine, and the only articles from her trousseau that had made it into the lucky piece of luggage that managed to arrive in Greece along with her.

Afterward, she studied herself in the mirrored door of the closet with a critical eye. Turning sideways, she sucked in her stomach until her belly was concave and the bottom of her rib cage became visible. Gee, as long as she didn't breathe, she sported measurements that the pinups girls of the 1940s would have envied. But Darcie was fond of breathing, so she let out her breath on a gusty sigh. Goodbye twenty-four-inch waist.

Still, she liked her curves and the muscle tone she'd

managed to carve into them thanks to six months' worth of grueling workouts with the personal trainer from hell. She reached into the closet for the dress she'd just purchased. She had to admit it showed off all of her assets to their greatest advantage.

Since the evening's dinner was at someone's home, Nerina had suggested a more casual wrap dress in a soft jersey fabric the color of ripe peaches. Both the color and the cut flattered Darcie. Best of all, she could pair it with flat shoes she already owned, saving her a second purchase. Nerina also had been generous on the price, declaring the garment on sale even though it was not marked as such.

"Enjoy your evening," she'd said as Darcie left the shop.

Looking at herself in the mirror now, Darcie grinned. Oh, she planned to.

Peach was his new favorite color, Nick decided, when Darcie stepped out of the elevator into the hotel lobby. As he eyed her curves, the air backed up in his lungs. The reaction wasn't entirely unpleasant, but it was unsettling and rare when it came to women. Except for this woman. Around Darcie, he couldn't seem to catch his breath at all.

From the first moment he'd spied her in the airport, he'd found himself drawn to her, interested in a way that he'd initially assumed was purely the result of sexual attraction. He'd gone on instinct when he'd approached her and offered his assistance. He'd followed his gut again when he'd come to her earlier in the day, asking a favor. Nick didn't regret his impulses, but he knew a moment of panic when she smiled at him now and his mouth went dry.

"I hope I'm dressed all right. I wasn't sure what to wear," she said.

"You look lovely." He kept his gaze locked on her face,

not trusting himself to take in those curves a second time without touching them.

"Thank you."

A pair of glossed lips parted in a smile that was nearly impossible to resist. He bit back a groan and asked, "Are you ready?"

"I am."

This time, instead of a Porsche, Nick was driving a 1965 Shelby Cobra.

"Very iconic," she murmured of the cobalt-blue car that sported twin white stripes up its hood and down its trunk. "One of the most sought-after cars as I recall from fact-checking an article about one. Is it the real deal?"

"If you are asking if it is one of the ten special racing editions, yes."

"Signed by Carroll Shelby?"

"Of course." Once again, Nick appreciated the depth of her knowledge. A woman who spoke car. He'd never met one before.

"I'm almost afraid to sit in it," she told him when he opened the door for her. "This baby goes for what? A couple hundred thousand American dollars?"

"Closer to three."

"Well, there, you've put my mind at ease," she replied dryly.

Nick chuckled. "Get in." Since the car had no roof and only a low, curving windshield, he handed her a scarf. "For your hair."

"Very thoughtful. Thank you. I feel Grace Kelly-ish. Or I would if I were a platinum blonde with classical features and a slimmer build."

"There's nothing wrong with your hair color, features or your...build."

She sent him a sideways smile. It sounded like she said, "I could get used to you."

The drive to his grandmother's house was relatively short. Still, as they cruised through the city, Nick used the time to prep Darcie on his life, starting with the basics such as his age and education.

"I have not told them very much about you."

"That's because you don't know very much about me," she pointed out.

"I am eager to remedy that." His tone hinted at something much more intimate than a family dinner. "I have told them that you are American and that we have not known one another for long. That way, they will not expect us to have all of the answers."

Besides, the sexual chemistry between the two of them was very real and would go a long way to making their relationship plausible in his family's eyes.

Darcie was nodding. "All right. So, how did we meet?"

"I think we should keep it simple and as close to truthful as possible. I do not usually lie to my family." He shifted his attention from the road to her when he added, "I do not usually lie to anyone."

"I figured that. Same goes for me." She took a deep breath. "So, we met in an airport."

"Let's make it Newark."

"I saw you across a crowded room, our eyes met and it was magic." She laughed, but something about her assessment struck Nick as disturbingly accurate.

"How about if we just say I offered to give you a ride when yours did not show?" He turned, found himself lost in the same blue eyes that had sucked him in across the airport terminal and added, "I was only too happy to come to the aid of a beautiful woman."

"The only problem with that is I do not live in New York City, but upstate in Buffalo."

"You were in New York on business then."

She nibbled her lip. "There's not much travel involved in my line of work. Not like yours. I can check facts over the phone or by computer. I've never had to hop a plane to do my job. Not that I wouldn't mind."

"On holiday then?"

"I guess that's believable."

"Have you ever been to New York?"

"Once. It was right after I graduated from high school. I went with my friend Becky and her family. We stayed at a hotel near Times Square and took in a Broadway show." Her smile was wide and nostalgic. "I loved it."

"The show or the city?"

"Both. All of that energy. I felt energized, too."

Nick heard awe in her voice and understood it. That was how he'd felt the first time he'd visited New York—absolutely blown away by the mania, yet eager to be part of it, too. Athens was hardly a small town, either in population or in feel, but no other place Nick had traveled, which he did extensively for business, compared to New York.

"You will have to visit again. I would be happy to show you around."

He meant it, he realized with a start. He could see her in his adopted city, enjoying the herb-crusted salmon at his favorite restaurant, sipping coffee at a sidewalk café near Central Park, window-shopping on Fifth Avenue. Most disturbing, Nick could picture Darcie in his apartment—his quiet and at times lonely retreat from the bustle of the city—curled up on his couch with a glass of wine in her hand, smiling at him in invitation.

She was smiling at him now when she replied, "Maybe I will."

He swallowed and forced his attention to the least erotic thing he could think of. "Tell me about your family. Do they also live in Buffalo?"

"For the most part. I have three sisters. Two older, one younger, all of them married. They're scattered in the suburbs with their husbands and kids, driving minivans and carpooling to soccer games and gymnastic classes."

"But not you."

"To my mother's everlasting regret."

"And your father? What does he think of your situation?"

"He tells me there's plenty of time to get married, have kids and buy a minivan." She frowned then. "But..."

"But?"

"He thinks I'm wasting my talent at my current job," she admitted quietly.

"Are you?"

Darcie made a sound that was halfway between a laugh and a sigh. "That's the subject for a very long conversation. Right now, I think we should stick to the basics."

She was right, of course, but Nick was too curious about her to let the matter drop. "What talent is it that your father feels you are wasting?"

"I have a degree in journalism from Buffalo State University. I enjoyed feature writing. Some of my professors told me I had a flair for it. My plan was to work at a newspaper and once I had enough decent clips—"

"Clips?"

"Copies of articles I'd written. Once I had enough of those, I was going to apply for a job at one of the large women's magazines headquartered in New York."

"So, you wanted to come to the big city?"

"I did," she admitted on a shy smile. "Once upon a time I thought I could make a name for myself in publishing."

"But?"

The smile vanished. Darcie shrugged. "Something came up and then the fact-checking job at *Automobile Enthusiasts Monthly* came along."

"Do you ever do any writing for that magazine? You certainly know enough about cars to do a credible job of it."

"The editor has let me do a couple of blurbs about upcoming car cruises, but nothing meaty or in-depth. He either tackles those himself—it's a small publication—or he farms them out to a freelancer. It doesn't hurt that the freelancer is a poker buddy." She sighed. "So, I check facts."

The more she said, the more questions Nick had. He contented himself by asking the one that cut straight to the heart of the matter.

"Do you enjoy your work, Darcie?"

"I suppose." She shrugged. "It pays the bills."

A tepid and telling answer, in Nick's opinion.

"You should do something you feel passionately about. Otherwise, what is the point?"

"I guess you would know, since you're obviously passionate about your work."

He glanced over and waited until he was sure he had her full attention. "I am passionate about much more than my work."

Nick's frank reply and the accompanying intimate smile sent a spurt of pure lust coursing through Darcie's veins. The excitement churning away inside frightened her a little. It was so foreign. It seemed forbidden. But it wasn't, she reminded herself. She was a single woman, a consenting adult. Heck, if she were being truthful, she was a parched patch of desert desperate for a good dousing of rain. Bring on the storm.

"If you continue to look at me like that, I will be tempted to forego dinner and return to your hotel instead," Nick told her. Once again, his words were blunt. His smile bordered on sinful.

She called herself a chicken, but decided to play it safe.

"Sorry, I was just thinking about…all of the changes that have occurred in my life recently. Maybe more are in order." Warming to the notion, she added, "God knows, the timing couldn't be better. I need to find a new place to live. Why not a new job, too?"

It wasn't as if anything tied her to *Automobile Enthusiasts Monthly*. The pay was mediocre, the benefits were crap. She'd only taken the position after she and Tad became serious. At the time, with some help from him, she'd convinced herself that a career in New York was a pipe dream. Settling down in Buffalo with reliable if tedious employment and a future with Tad—those were what had mattered, what she had wanted most.

"You are at a crossroads," Nick said. Up ahead, the light turned red and he slowed the Shelby to a stop.

Darcie gestured with her hand. "It's really more like this busy intersection, but with no working traffic light."

"Ah, then you need to take care in getting to the other side."

Treading carefully, that was how she'd spent the past several years. Feeling reckless now, she said, "Or I could just run like hell and hope for the best. After all, we've established that I am adventurous."

"I like your style." Nick's hand left the gearshift to caress her cheek. He was leaning toward her, eyes hooded with unmistakable intent, when a horn blasted behind them.

"The light is green," she said, suppressing a laugh.

"Yes. A green light. I believe I got that very impression."

The car shot forward. Darcie's pulse lurched as if trying to catch up. The scarf was in no danger of blowing off, but she pulled it snugger around her head, just to have something to do with her hands.

"Let's talk about you."

"All right. You know what I do for a living. You also know I have a brother who is to be married."

"A younger brother. Pieter."

"Very good. You pay close attention to details."

"It's what I do." She shrugged. "I check facts for a living, remember?"

"Or you did."

The seed, so recently planted, seemed to be taking root. But she forced herself to focus on the present. "Tell me about Pieter. How old is he? What's he like? Are you close?"

A muscle ticked in Nick's jaw, although when he spoke, his tone bordered on blasé. "He is a year my junior. As boys, we did everything together. Now...he works with our father at his shop. They are electricians by trade."

"The family business?"

Nick nodded. "My father had hoped I would follow in his footsteps as well."

"But you had other interests."

"Yes."

One syllable said without regret but full of sadness. More family expectations, Darcie decided. Hoping to lighten his mood, she shifted the subject. "Why don't you tell me about Pieter's fiancée?"

That muscle ticked in Nick's jaw again. "Selene."

The wind rushed past in the open car, but the tension grew thicker. "Um, that's a pretty name."

He snorted. "We grew up together, the three of us." Nick paused before adding, "Selene and I used to date."

Darcie blinked, too surprised to apply tact when she said, "You dated the woman your brother is marrying?"

"It would be more accurate to say that my brother is marrying a woman I dated," he replied tersely.

"Oh." More like *uh-oh*. Darcie had stepped into something unpleasant, and she had no clue how to scrape it gracefully off her shoe.

"You are wondering if I am heartbroken."

"Are you?" she asked bluntly.

"It was over a long time ago."

Nick might not be heartbroken—and the jury was still out on that as far as she was concerned—but Darcie didn't think it was as over as he claimed it to be. She heard another emotion in his tone. Anger? Betrayal? If it truly was over, he would feel nothing. She wanted to ask why he and Selene had broken up, but she sensed that topic wasn't open for discussion.

She said quietly, "It has to be awkward."

"It is."

Did this mean Nick was on the rebound, too? She wasn't sure how she felt about that or even if she had the right to feel anything. They had been driving in silence for a couple of minutes, when something occurred to her.

"Um, speaking of awkward, will Selene and Pieter be at dinner tonight?"

As it was, Darcie had enough to worry about what with convincing his parents and grandmother that she and Nick were an item without adding bad blood and an old lovers' triangle to the mix. Thankfully, Nick shook his head.

"They have other plans. Some last-minute meeting with the caterer about changes to one of the side dishes. Apparently, a cousin of the bride has a severe peanut allergy."

"Oh, thank God." Darcie closed her eyes and grimaced. "Not about the allergy. Those can be deadly. Anaphylactic shock and all. But—"

"I know exactly what you mean." His dry laughter served to put her at ease.

A few minutes later, they arrived at a two-story white stucco home surrounded by lush, terraced gardens.

"We're here."

Showtime, Darcie thought, as she removed the scarf and checked her appearance in the rearview mirror.

"You look beautiful," he assured her.

Even so, nerves fluttered in her belly. She offered up a prayer that in addition to passing parental inspection, she wouldn't humiliate herself by getting sick.

"This is my grandmother's house, but my mother and father live just there."

He pointed to the home next door that was similar in size and appearance and whose yard was equally well-landscaped. Concentrating on the details helped quell her nerves. As limited as her knowledge of plants was, she recognized geraniums spilling from the pots near the front door, as well as near the iron railing that girded a second-story terrace. And even without the assistance of a breeze, she could smell the heady scent of roses.

"Wow. Your mother and grandmother must have green thumbs. Everything looks so, well, *green*. My mom is like that. And my sisters. They can grow anything, anywhere. As near as I can tell, my thumb is black."

"Black?" He took her hands, studied the digits in question. "They look normal to me."

"It's just a saying. It means I'm a plant killer, which is why the only plant I own is a ficus whose leaves are made of plastic. There's no chance of killing that sucker."

"I see," Nick said patiently.

No, he didn't, because there was no point to this conversation, except for stalling. Darcie was babbling like an idiot, but she couldn't seem to stop herself. More words tumbled out. "Although the ficus still looks pathetic thanks to Rufus."

Nick's lips twitched. "The cat you referred to as the spawn of Satan?"

"That's the one. He used it as a scratching post."

Nick got out and came around the car to open Darcie's door. "Come." Suddenly he seemed so formidable, as though he were prepared for battle. The sudden change from playful to guarded did nothing to settle Darcie's nerves.

He led her to the door, entered without knocking. This might have been his grandmother's house, but he didn't stand on formality. She liked that. The foyer opened into a living room with a fireplace. It was a comfortable room, a place that invited one to sit and relax. Darcie wished she could, but she was wound up as tight as a spring. From the rear of the house, she could hear voices, although she couldn't make out anything that was being said since it was in Greek. She heard Nick's name mentioned and then she thought she heard her own. When she glanced at him, his expression was apologetic.

"They say they are eager to meet you."

Darcie doubted his translation was complete or completely accurate.

He took her hand. "This way."

The mingled scents of spices and roasting meat wafting from the kitchen should have had her mouth watering, but it was dry as sawdust. She stopped walking.

"I need another minute," she whispered and sucked in a deep breath.

"You are nervous. I understand."

Did he? It wasn't only her part in the deception that had her worried, but what his family would think of her. Her old insecurities bubbled up before she could stop them. What if they found her as lacking as Evelyn had?

"You will be fine."

"Fine," she repeated, feeling anything but.

"It is only one meal."

Yes, but it felt like her last supper.

"Darcie." Nick framed her face with his hands. His palms were warm, the pads of his thumbs slightly calloused as they brushed over her cheeks. "You…"

Whatever else he said, and she thought it might have been in Greek, was lost to the rushing in her ears. Besides, words, no matter what the language, were superfluous. He was going to kiss her again. That much came through loud and clear. And she wanted him to. So much so that she didn't bother to wait for him to lean in and claim her mouth. She clasped the back of his neck and closed the gap between them herself.

She'd always been a fan of fireworks, though it had been a very long time since she'd experienced any. This kind lit her up inside until she was sure her skin glowed from the heat. Someone moaned. She was pretty sure the sound came from her. Regardless, Nick took the opportunity to change the angle of their mouths. His hands no longer framed her face. His fingers splayed over the small of her back, exerting subtle pressure that brought her flush against his hard chest.

A woman's voice cut through the haze of hormones.

"This must be Darcie."

They sprung apart. Fireworks fizzled until they were but pesky smoke. Way to make a first impression, Darcie thought, giving herself a mental slap. Nick, meanwhile, offered the sort of charmingly sheepish smile that probably had helped him out of plenty of scrapes as a boy.

"Mama. My apologies. I seem to have gotten carried away."

"Yes. That much I could see for myself," she replied dryly.

But she was smiling. And so was the older woman standing just behind her in the doorway.

In heavily accented English, Nick's *yiayia* said, "Manners, Nikolos, manners. Introduce us."

He rubbed his hands together. "Of course. Darcie Hayes, this is my grandmother, Sophia Pappas, and my mother, Thea Costas."

Hands were shaken, greetings exchanged. Darcie knew she was being sized up. Funny, but some of her earlier nervousness had evaporated. Nick's mother and grandmother were curious about her, that much was very clear. But she sensed no antipathy, no animosity. She felt welcome if not accepted. And that was before his grandmother slid one of her boney arms around Darcie's waist and propelled her toward the kitchen.

"Come. I will pour the wine. You will tell us about yourself. Start with your ancestors. Might there be a chance some of your people came from Greece?"

CHAPTER FIVE

NICK'S FATHER ARRIVED just before the meal was served. By then, Darcie's nerves had calmed substantially. It helped that while seated in the kitchen watching Thea and Sophia finish the preparations she'd polished off a glass of a lovely dry red wine.

She refused a refill when Nick would have poured her one. It wouldn't do to get snockered. But she told them, "This was very good."

"It is bottled by Nick's uncle, my brother, and his sons," Thea said proudly. "They have a small vineyard in Thrace."

"Nick is the only one of his generation to leave Greece to work," Sophia lamented. "We keep hoping he will return for good one day."

"Yiayia," he said.

"What? I only say what is true. That is what we all hope will happen. Is it not, Thea?"

His mother flushed and was saved from answering by Nick's father, who said as he entered the kitchen, "He is here now. Let us enjoy our time together."

The older man wasn't as tall as Nick, but his shoulders were just as broad. Age had added more girth to his waist, deep lines to the corners of his eyes and gray hair to his temples. But he remained a handsome man. This is how Nick would look in thirty years' time, Darcie thought. Warmth spread through her. She chalked it up to the wine.

"This is my father, George Costas," Nick said.

"Darcie Hayes." When she would have shaken his hand, George kissed both of her cheeks.

"She is prettier than Danika." He winked at Nick.

"Danika?" Darcie mouthed.

"I will explain later," Nick mumbled.

"Stop flirting, *Baba*, and go wash up," Thea said with an exaggerated shake of her head. "Dinner is ready."

They ate *alfresco*, seated around a table under a pergola in Yiayia's backyard. Vine-covered trellises lined the pergola's sides, offering shade from the late day sun. The center of the table was heaped with enough food to feed twice as many people.

Darcie smoothed a napkin over her lap. "Everything looks wonderful, Mrs. Costas and Mrs. Pappas."

"Call me Yiayia. Everyone does."

"And you may call me Thea," Nick's mother said, passing Darcie a platter of sliced lamb. "You are not a vegetarian, I hope. A lot of young people are nowadays."

"No." Even if Darcie had been, the delicious-smelling meat would have tempted her to take a bite.

"That is good," Yiayia said. "Nick likes red meat."

"True." Thea nodded. "But he will fly home for dinner on a Palm Sunday if I promise to make *bakaliaros tiganitos*."

At Darcie's perplexed expression, he explained, "It is a salt-cured cod that my mother then batters and deep fries. It is very tasty, but it is the dipping sauce she makes to go with it that has me booking my flight."

"Here, we are so close to the ocean that the fish is fresh and plentiful," Yiayia said.

"Manhattan is next to the Atlantic," he pointed out patiently and Darcie got the feeling this was a long-standing argument.

"It is settled," George offered. "Water and fish are everywhere."

But Yiayia wasn't done. "Do they even know how to make *bakaliaros tiganitos* in America?"

"I will look on the menu at the next Greek restaurant I visit."

Sophia shrugged. "It does not matter. They will not cook it as well as your mama does. I taught her, just as my mother taught me. Just as your mother will teach your future wife." She glanced slyly at Darcie.

George apparently didn't get the memo about playing it coy. "Maybe you could teach Darcie, Thea."

Everyone at the table turned and gaped at him. Nick was the first to recover. There was a gleam in his eye when he said, "I do like Mama's *bakaliaros tiganitos.*"

"Nick likes *all* of his mama's cooking," George said with a hearty laugh. "He gets that from me."

"If he is not careful, he will get this, too." Thea patted her husband's stomach. More laughter followed, chasing away a bit of the strain.

"If you would like, I could share some of my recipes with you," Thea said to Darcie, "including the one for *bakaliaros tiganitos.* It is not so hard to make, but you must soak the fish overnight or it will be too salty."

"Thank you. I would like that."

"Are you a good cook?" Sophia asked.

"Um, I…" Darcie had mastered the art of microwaving in college, and she knew how to whip up staples such as grilled cheese and spaghetti, as long as the sauce for the latter came from a jar. But her culinary skills didn't go much beyond that since, at Evelyn's insistence, Darcie and Tad had eaten most of their meals at his mother's. In Darcie's new home, wherever that might be, she was going to take the time to learn. "I plan to be."

Yiayia's eyes narrowed. Clearly, that answer hadn't won Darcie any points.

"Do you cook for Nick?"

Before she could formulate a response, he explained, "We eat out whenever Darcie comes to town."

"And where does she sleep when she comes to town?" Yiayia asked pointedly.

Darcie felt her face flame, but Nick took the question in stride. "She sleeps in a bed," he replied without specifying whose. Since his grin left little doubt, she kicked him under the table.

Earlier, in the kitchen, they had discussed how Darcie and Nick met. Now, the topic turned to what she did for a living, what her family was like and the names of her siblings, brothers-in-law, nephews and nieces. Yiayia, of course, snuck in a question about how many children Darcie wanted. By the time coffee and dessert were served, Yiayia had determined two things. One, Darcie was too thin and, two, she must have some Greek in her, if only because she liked the strong coffee.

"I like the cake, too," Darcie noted after taking a bite. It was topped with powdered sugar and lightly toasted almonds. "It's delicious. What's it called?"

"Revani," Yiayia said.

"Revani," Darcie repeated. Or so she thought. But Yiayia was shaking her head.

"No, no, no. Re-vah-*nee.*"

"Emphasis on the last syllable," Nick supplied.

Darcie tried the word again, this time earning his grandmother's nod of approval.

"I make this special for Nick. I will be sure to give you the recipe so you can make it, too."

Darcie sent him a smile and asked, "Is this another favorite of yours?"

But it wasn't Nick who answered.

"My brother is fond of all sweet things."

Pieter stood just outside the door that led from the house. At least, Darcie assumed the man was Pieter. The family resemblance was there in the shape of his eyes and the athletic build. And if he was Pieter, that would make the woman standing beside him Selene.

OMG!

Darcie set down her fork and blotted her mouth on the napkin. Then she sat up straighter in her chair and sucked in her stomach. Selene was slender and petite. Darcie felt like an Amazon in comparison. And the other woman was drop-dead gorgeous with high cheekbones, delicately arched brows and sleek black hair. In short, she was Aphrodite incarnate. A glance at Nick confirmed what Darcie already knew: if he was over what had happened, he was doing a poor job showing it. His eyes had turned as hard as stone.

"Pieter! Selene!" Thea smiled nervously. "We did not think you would be here."

"We finished our appointment with the caterer early and thought we would stop by for cake."

"How did you know about the cake?" Nick asked.

"Yiayia called earlier and mentioned it."

All eyes cut to Yiayia.

"I am an old woman," she muttered with the wave of an arthritic hand. "I cannot remember what I say, who I say it to."

Half of Pieter's mouth rose in a resigned smile. "The only reason you are here is because you did not think that we would be. I guess I was foolish to hope."

Nick said nothing, but that muscle started to tick in his jaw again.

"It does not matter. I am glad to see you, Nick. We both are." Pieter curved his arm around Selene's shoulders and she offered a tentative smile.

The tension built along with the silence. Darcie was the one who breached it.

"Pieter and Selene. Nick has told me so much about you both. It's so nice to finally meet you."

"And you are?" Pieter asked.

"Darcie Hayes. Nick's...Nick's girlfriend."

She'd already stepped in this mess with one foot. Why not both?

"You played your part well this evening," Nick told Darcie once the two of them were in the Shelby and heading back to her hotel.

At times he had forgotten their bargain and actually enjoyed himself. That was until Pieter and Selene's arrival. Seeing them together never put Nick in a good mood. This evening it had been tolerable. He had Darcie to thank for that.

"You weren't half-bad yourself," she told him. "If your car auction business doesn't pan out you might consider a career on Broadway."

She smiled, but her tone didn't match the lighthearted comment.

"Is something wrong, Darcie?"

She fussed with the scarf's knot under her chin. "Your family is really nice, Nick. I enjoyed meeting them all."

"And they enjoyed meeting you," he replied warily.

"I don't like lying to them, Nick. Even if most of our lies were ones of omission."

He nodded. "Most of them."

The one that stood out had come from Darcie at the end of dinner: *I'm Nick's girlfriend.*

Upon hearing that, Pieter's expression had reflected not only surprise, but also happiness and hope. More than anything else from the evening, it was the hope that bothered Nick's conscience.

"Sophia is something else." Darcie chuckled. "But she only has your best interests at heart. All of them do."

Nick saw his brother's hopeful expression again only to banish it. "If that is so, they should be satisfied now. You made quite an impression on them."

"I suppose." She cleared her throat. Her tone was tentative when she said, "Your brother seems nice. Selene, too."

Nick made a noncommittal sound and concentrated on driving, hoping Darcie would drop the subject.

She didn't.

"They both seemed genuinely happy for you...us...well, you know what I mean."

"Guilty consciences looking for absolution," he muttered. But was that the cause? He decided to change the subject. "Are you really going to try the recipes my mother and grandmother gave you? Or did you just say that to humor them?"

"Oh, no. I meant it. I'm not sure where I am going to get salt-cured cod, but everything else looks pretty manageable."

"They love to fiddle in the kitchen. I think they should have their own television program."

"Cooking with Thea and Sophia," Darcie offered. They both laughed. "I would watch it. I really do want to learn. I know the basics, but for the past six years, we pretty much ate all of our dinners at Evelyn's house."

"Evelyn?"

"Tad's mother," Darcie said quietly.

Nick glanced sideways. Darcie was staring at her hands,

which were now folded in her lap. "What is a Tad? Or should I ask who?"

She ran a tongue over her teeth. "He's my former fiancé."

Nick nearly blew through a red light. He brought the Shelby to a stop to the protest of skidding tires. Giving Darcie his full attention now, he asked, "How recently former?"

She wrinkled her nose. "Pretty recent. We were supposed to get married last Saturday, but I called it off the week before."

The breath left Nick's lungs in a gust as he added two and two together and came up with four. "He is the reason you are now looking for a new place to live."

"Yes. Tad got the cat and the condo in our breakup. I got…Greece."

Nick's eyebrows shot up in surprise. "So this trip was to be your…"

"Honeymoon," she finished for him. Her smile was tight, her laughter apologetic as he absorbed a second bombshell that he hadn't seen coming.

He should say something, he thought, although "sorry" didn't feel right, even if what she had just shared must have been painful. Endings always were. Briefly, he considered telling her about Selene and Pieter. She probably would welcome a little quid pro quo under the circumstances. But the words stuck in his throat. They drove the rest of the way in silence.

"Stop here," she said when they reached her hotel. "There's no need to park and walk me inside."

He wanted to disagree. But the evening was over and it was time to say good-night. It was just as well. His emotions were all over the place. He didn't care for the confusion. One thing he knew for sure, however, was that his interest in Darcie had not diminished one iota.

"What time shall we meet tomorrow?" At her puzzled

expression he reminded her, "I said I would act as your tour guide. I intend to live up to my end of the bargain."

"Oh. I'll leave the time up to you."

"I am an early riser, but how about nine o'clock?"

"All right. We can meet in the lobby again, if that works for you."

He nodded. "Where would you like to go?"

"The Parthenon."

Nick smiled. "Then the Parthenon it is." When she reached for the door handle, he said, "Aren't you forgetting something?"

She glanced around, her expression uncertain. "What?"

"A kiss good-night." Unable to resist, he leaned over the gearshift and captured her mouth. As the kiss deepened, he regretted the car's bucket seats. "Sleep well, Darcie," Nick said, pulling back.

"Right. As if…" she muttered, getting out.

The phone in Darcie's hotel room trilled at an ungodly hour. She pushed the pillow off her face and, eyes still closed, felt around on the nightstand until she found the receiver.

"'Lo," she mumbled.

"Are you alone?" It was Becky.

Darcie rubbed her eyes. "Yes, I'm alone. Why wouldn't I be alone?"

"You were supposed to call after your date with Mr. Tall, Greek and Gorgeous," her friend reminded her. "When you didn't, well, I thought…"

No need for Becky to fill in the blank. Darcie's imagination had been busy doing that very thing for most of the night.

"Nick dropped me off at the hotel just after ten. I fell asleep soon after. Alone. Sorry I didn't call. I was just too tired. Jet lag and all." It was a handy excuse, but not the whole truth. The whole truth was Darcie hadn't wanted to examine more closely the evening, its ending or the insane attraction she felt for the man in question.

But Becky wasn't giving her an out this time. "So, how was it?"

"Nice. I had a good time."

"Nice? A good time? Sheesh, Darcie. I called for details. Not the abridged version you save for your mother."

Darcie chuckled at that. "My mother is never going to hear any version, abridged or otherwise, where Nick is concerned. I think she still may be holding out hope that Tad and I will get back together and there will be no need to deal with the stack of gifts she promised she would help me return."

"Speaking of Tad, I ran in to him at our favorite coffee shop."

"Tad doesn't like coffee." He complained the beverage stained his teeth.

"I know. Even stranger, he made a point of coming over and saying hello to me."

That was surprising. Tad and Becky didn't like one another, but over the years, they had brokered a truce of sorts—a truce Darcie would have assumed null and void now that the wedding had been called off.

"He asked if I'd heard from you."

"He did not."

"Swear. He wanted to know how you were doing."

"What did you say?"

"I told him we'd talked and that you were having a fabulous time with a hot Greek man."

"You did not!" Darcie exclaimed.

"Okay, those weren't my exact words. But I did tell him that his bargain trip had turned out to be a bust and that you'd been stranded at the airport until a nice man came to your aid. Tad said he'd been trying to reach you on your cell. For that matter, I have, too."

Darcie glanced toward her discarded purse on the chair in the corner. "I silenced the ringer before dinner with Nick's family last night. I haven't turned it back on. Did Tad say why he was calling?"

"No. He looked, well, like he was kind of lost without you."

"Tad?" Darcie couldn't help but be surprised. "I didn't think he would notice my absence. He still has his mother, after all." She shook her head. "That was mean. I don't want him to be unhappy."

"That's because you're a nice person, Darcie. Too nice. Tad took advantage of that. So, are you going to call him? I don't think you should."

"I won't. At least not until I return home." When her friend started to object, Darcie pointed out, "We have to talk, if only so he knows where to forward my mail. Besides, I'm the one who called off the wedding, Becks. That makes Tad the injured party."

A snort came over the line. "Do yourself a favor, and don't feel too sorry for him. Remember, he's the reason you found yourself stranded in Greece."

"Yes, but that's turning out okay." A grin spread over Darcie's face.

"I knew it! Tell me everything about last night. And remember, no skimping when it comes to details."

She still wound up giving Becky an abridged version of events, leaving out completely the arrival of Pieter and Selene at the end of dinner, and the awkward tension that had followed. Darcie didn't want to more closely examine the feelings Nick stirred in her. It was easier just to leave it at mutual attraction. The timing for anything else was completely wrong—apparently for both of them.

As their conversation wound up, Becky said, "Have fun exploring the Parthenon. Hey, take a picture of Nick with your phone and send it to me. I want to see your hot man for myself."

After they said goodbye, Darcie had less than an hour to get ready. The elevator doors slid open at the lobby with five minutes to spare. When she stepped out, the hot man in question was standing to one side of the reception desk. His mouth curved into an appreciative smile that turned her insides to mush. With one look, he made her feel beautiful, desirable and once again ready to toss caution to the wind. That was enough, she decided.

"Kalimera su," she said when she reached him.

His brows rose.

"One of the few Greek phrases I know. Did I say it right?"

"You did. Good morning to you, too." He kissed her cheeks, lingering long enough to make the greeting less platonic. "You look lovely, by the way."

"You do, too. Not lovely, but…" Good enough to gobble up in a T-shirt that fit snugly across his chest. She coughed and forced her gaze back to his. "Um, ready to take in the sights?"

By way of an answer, he took her hand.

Growing up in Athens, Nick had been to the Parthenon dozens of times. He experienced it anew seeing it through Darcie's eyes. She was in total awe.

"It's hard to believe something built more than four hundred years before the birth of Christ is still standing."

"Not all of it is," Nick pointed out.

"But enough of it remains to hint at its former grandeur," she argued. "Those columns are massive. Haven't you ever wondered how the ancient Greeks managed to get them up without modern tools and machinery?"

He grinned. "I am now."

"I'm serious, Nick."

"So I see."

"There's very little in the United States that dates back more than a couple hundred years. Yet here stands a temple, a stunning example of Doric-style architecture, I might add, that was designed by Phidias to honor Athena, the patron goddess of your city, and constructed more than two thousand years ago."

"Your knowledge of the Parthenon is impressive," he said.

"I read about it." She started to laugh. "Over there."

Nick turned to find a large sign listing the same facts Darcie had just spouted. He started to laugh, too, and then pulled her into his arms. He didn't let her go. Both of them sobered.

"I like your sense of humor," he said.

"It's one of my better attributes."

"I can think of other attributes that I prefer even more." He slid his hands down her back and, even though he wanted to place them elsewhere, he forced them to stop at her waist. They were in public, after all, and surrounded by camera-toting tourists.

"You must mean my eyes." She batted the lids. The eyes in question were laughing at him. "I've been told they're a pretty color."

"You are enjoying this," he accused.

"Enjoying what?" she asked a little too innocently. "I don't know what you mean."

"I do like your eyes," he agreed. "But they aren't what kept me awake last night." As intended, his bald assertion wiped the smile from Darcie's face. Then he asked, "How did you sleep? Did you toss and turn?"

"I…I…" She swallowed.

"That is what I thought."

Those blue eyes narrowed. "That's not fair."

"Why?"

"I did toss and turn, but I'm still suffering from jet lag."

"You are full of excuses."

"It's true."

"All right. I have a cure for that." His voice was low and for the briefest moment his hips bumped against hers as he spoke. "Would you like to know what it is?"

"Right now? Right here?" She gave a panicked glance around.

Nick brushed the hair back from her cheek and leaned closer. His lips purposely grazed her ear when he whispered, "Warm milk."

"Warm—" Darcie dissolved in a fit of laughter that drew curious stares from passersby. When she composed herself, she accused, "You set me up."

"I cannot be responsible for the thoughts you entertain." His voice dropped an octave. "Although I would not mind hearing what they are."

She put a hand on his chest and playfully pushed him backward half a step. "Oh, no. I'm not walking into a trap a second time."

Just that quickly, he erased the distance she'd created, and pulled her close. "Now I *really* want to hear those thoughts. Over dinner, perhaps? Say yes."

"Well, when you put it that way. Yes."

CHAPTER SIX

NICK CHANGED HIS mind several times before settling on a restaurant. Even then he wasn't sure he'd made the right choice. He had no doubt Darcie would enjoy the food and the ambience. They were what made it so difficult to get a table at Moscophilero…unless one had a long history with the owner, as Nick did. But the restaurant's location gave him pause. It was in Piraeus and, as such, much closer to his house above the harbor than anything in Athens would be. Within fifteen minutes of his paying the check, he and Darcie could be ensconced in his living room sipping a nightcap. As for what they could be doing within an hour, that gave him pause.

Where was this heading? Where did he want it to head? Such questions had never arisen with the other women he'd dated, but Darcie was…special. In addition to turning him on to an extent he'd never experienced, she also brought out his protective instincts. Add in her recently ended engagement and Nick didn't want to rush her. But he did want her. So, he needed to be sure they were both after the same thing: a mutually satisfying, albeit short-term, sexual relationship. Recriminations afterward wouldn't do.

Ultimately, he decided to tell her their destination and see if she would prefer to stay in Athens proper.

"I wouldn't mind seeing the seaside," she told him when they met in the hotel lobby.

Her assent did little to quell his nerves. But when they stepped outside, her laughter did.

"Nick Costas, man of many cars. I never know what you'll be driving next." Her lips curved.

Earlier, when he'd taken Darcie to the Parthenon, he'd been driving an Aston Martin coupe. He liked to get behind the wheel of the automobiles he would be auctioning, especially those he purchased himself and for whom he had no specific collector in mind, to get a feel for how they handled. In this case, however, the cherry-red Jaguar roadster would never see the auction block. It belonged to him and had for the past few years. He kept it at his house in Greece for personal use. In New York, his vehicle of choice was a 1966 Corvette Sting Ray.

"You will get a prize if you know the year this car was manufactured," he said.

"Hmm. Let's see. Streamlined body and covered headlights." She pursed her lips and glanced inside. "Sunken floor pans. Four-speed manual gearbox." Straightening, she said, "I'm going to say it was built in nineteen sixty…five."

"You are close. Sixty-six."

She wrinkled her nose. "What would my prize have been?"

She had to ask. His body tightened, but he managed a casual shrug. "I was going to let you drive it."

"Then it's just as well I got the answer wrong," she told him on a laugh. "The steering wheel is on the wrong side of the car."

"For the United States," he agreed.

"That increases the value, of course, a fact of which I am sure you are aware."

He nodded, pleased by her astuteness and an idea niggled. He pushed it to the back burner. "Fewer than a thousand of the right-hand drive models were produced in 1966."

The restaurant was busy when they arrived. They were shown to their table in a prime location at the window that offered an unparalleled view of the harbor. The day was winding down, the sun starting to set. Boats, both commercial and pleasure craft, were heading in for the night.

"I could sit here all day," she murmured. "What is it about water that is so...compelling?"

Nick lifted his shoulders. He couldn't put it into words, but he understood what she meant. The view drew him. It always had. It was one of the things he missed when he was in Manhattan, and one of the reasons he knew he would never sell his home here, even though he did not spend very much time in it.

A black-vested waiter came by and took their beverage order. Darcie opted for a glass of white wine. Nick ordered the same. A moment later, the man was back with their drinks and a complimentary platter of olives, cheese and dense bread.

"Khristos sends his regards," the waiter said.

"Khristos?" Darcie asked once they were alone.

"The owner. He and I are old friends."

She lifted her glass of wine. "To old friends then."

Nick raised his glass as well, but he had a different toast in mind. "And to new friendships."

She smiled in agreement and clinked her glass against his.

"You know, even though I have only known you a short time, I do consider you a friend, Nick."

In the time it took her to say so, the word lost all of its appeal. "Merely a friend?"

"A very handsome one." She arched her brows. "Better?"

"A little. My ego thanks you."

Darcie selected an olive from the platter and popped it into her mouth. His started to water, only to go dry when she turned the question back around on him.

"What do you consider me? If your answer is a nuisance, feel free to make up something else. My ego will be every bit as appreciative as yours was."

Nick chuckled. "I suppose I should confess that initially I considered you a delightful distraction."

"That was when you offered me a ride from the airport." She nodded, selected another olive. Before popping it into her mouth she added, "Then you saw me as your ticket out of a tight spot with your mother and grandmother."

"A lovely ticket."

She batted her eyelashes comically and murmured her thanks. "And now, after spending the better part of the day touring ancient ruins with me, are we pals?"

Another time, Nick would have laughed. But he weighed her words carefully and then weighed his own. "Not by my definition, but English is my second language. The fact is, Darcie, friendship seems a rather bland term for us. Do you not agree?"

"What other term do you have in mind?"

"That is my dilemma. I have no other term." He sipped his wine. "I was hoping you might."

"Well, if we're being honest, I don't think platonic applies to our situation."

He agreed, of course, but was curious to hear Darcie's reasons. "Go on."

A couple blotches of color worked their way up from her neck until they flamed on her cheeks. "Speaking only for myself, I like kissing you. I'm pretty sure people who are merely friends don't   kiss—" she cleared her throat "—like that." She cleared her throat again. "Or enjoy it quite so much."

"We are attracted to one another," Nick agreed. "And I, too, like kissing you."

"My friend Becky would say that what you and I have going qualifies as a fling. Well, a baby fling, really, since we're not..."

Sleeping together went unspoken, but Darcie may as well have screamed it. Nick heard the words loud and clear and finished her thought with a silent *yet*.

He hid his grin behind the rim of his glass and sipped his wine. He liked Darcie's friend's assessment. After all, in addition to sex, *fling* implied impermanence. It bolstered his assumption that Darcie, who had so recently freed herself from her own betrothal, wasn't looking for true love and a lasting commitment any more than he was. She was after excitement, a little fun.

Still, he needed to be positive.

"And, if instead of this baby fling, we were to have a very adult one, what then?"

She moistened her lips. "I'm not sure I understand your question."

"What would you expect?"

The waiter picked that inopportune moment to return and take their dinner orders. Nick clenched his teeth and waited to hear Darcie's response.

"This is all very hypothetical," she began once they were alone again. "I'm not really the sort of woman who goes around having flings, especially of the adult variety."

"I never assumed otherwise," he hastened to assure her. "In fact, you might say that is the reason I am seeking clarity on the matter."

Her expression turned thoughtful. "First and foremost, I would expect the truth. I won't tolerate lies."

Her response surprised him a little. Even though it was none of his business, he asked, "Did your fiancé lie to you?"

"I'm sure he would say no." She pursed her lips, as if considering. "I think Tad lied to himself much more than he lied to me. He said I was the one he wanted to spend the rest of his life with, but, in the end, it wasn't going to be just the two of us."

Nick's brows shot up at that, but he kept his voice neutral when he asked, "What do you mean?"

"I wouldn't have been marrying just him. I would have been marrying his mother, too." The shiver that accompanied her words appeared involuntary rather than manufactured for effect.

"I gather that his mother did not like you."

"I wasn't good enough for her son. Tad's quite the catch. A *doctor*, you know." She emphasized the word in a way that Nick imagined other people had in speaking to Darcie. "But that doesn't change the fact that he's a world-class mama's boy."

"Obviously, I do not know Tad or his mother, but my guess is that no one would have been good enough for her son, even a woman as wonderful as you."

"Thanks." Darcie smiled. "And I know what you mean."

Did she? If so, Nick thought that might have been a recent development. Her uncertainty would explain why Darcie had been flustered by a simple compliment when he first met her.

She was saying, "Evelyn's fault-finding might not have been such a big issue if we hadn't spent so much time with her. Dinner practically every evening, church on Sundays. The last straw was when Tad started talking about adding another master suite on to her house instead of continuing to look for a house of our own after we got married."

"Pieter and Selene will live down the street from my parents, who, as you know, live next door to my grandmother."

"Next door and down the street are not the same as under

one roof with shared main living spaces. I always felt on guard around Evelyn. I couldn't slouch without hearing her comment on my poor posture."

"Tad allowed this?"

"He has a blind spot a mile wide where his mother is concerned."

"Then he got what he deserved," Nick said. "He lost you, but gets to keep his mother."

Her lips twitched. "And don't forget Rufus. He's keeping the cat, too."

"Good riddance, spawn of Satan."

Darcie laughed.

They were both quiet for a moment. Then Nick said, "I am sorry that things didn't work out."

Sympathy was expected, though Nick actually felt no such thing. If Darcie were now a married woman, they never would have met, and he still would be dodging his family's matchmaking attempts. His relief was selfish, his reasons rooted in his current situation, he assured himself. They had nothing to do with that tug of attraction and something less definable that he felt when he was with Darcie.

"Well, I'm not sorry. I mean, I'm sorry that I let things go on for so long and that Becky wound up shelling out good money for a tangerine gown that she isn't going to be able to wear anyplace except maybe a costume party." Darcie shook her head on a laugh. "God, I must sound so cold."

"Not at all. More like honest," Nick said.

He appreciated honesty. And he appreciated her situation. A woman who had recently ended her engagement would not be looking for another relationship so soon. But...

"Getting back to our possible fling, in addition to honesty, what else would you expect?"

"I don't know. This is an awkward conversation."

"It is all hypothetical, remember?"

"Hypothetical or not, it's still awkward. As worldly and sophisticated as I'd like you to think I am, I'm…just not." She shrugged.

When she said things like that, his protective instincts kicked into high gear. For all of her bravado and flippant comments, she was vulnerable and uncertain. She could be hurt. Hell, she already had been by a man who claimed to love her, but had allowed his own mother to belittle her.

Darcie shifted in her seat. "Maybe you should tell me what you would expect."

"Fair enough." He picked up his glass and took a drink, allowing the crisp white wine to bathe his tongue as he searched for the right words. "I would expect to have more dinners such as this one. I enjoy our conversations."

"And?"

"Well, like you, I would expect honesty."

"Of course." She nodded. "And?"

"Whatever were to happen naturally between us, it would be mutually agreed upon and enjoyed."

"A very diplomatic answer," she said.

"Something for both of us to think about."

Their entrées arrived then and the conversation turned to benign topics. Nick was eyeing the dessert menu, if only to prolong their evening, when Darcie said, "That was almost as good as the dinner your mom and grandmother made."

"I will be sure to pass along your compliment. You have room for dessert tonight, yes?"

She grinned. "I'm on vacation. I get to indulge." When he lifted a brow, she clarified, "In sweets."

They ordered coffee and two pieces of chocolate cake layered with a decadent mousse filling. The cake was delicious, but what made his mouth water was watching Darcie savor each bite.

He set his fork aside and, after taking a sip of coffee,

asked her, "Have you decided where I will be taking you tomorrow?"

"I was thinking the Temple of Zeus and Hadrian's Arch. That is if you have the time."

"I will *make* the time."

Darcie had blown her diet big-time with that delicious dessert, so it was a good thing the scrumptious man she'd spent the evening with came calorie-free. Still, if one of them had to go straight to her hips, she would rather it be Nick.

"You are smiling," the man in question noted as they returned to the hotel. "Care to share your thoughts?"

"No." She pressed her lips together tightly afterward to keep from smiling again.

"Ah." He nodded.

"*Ah* what?"

"There is no need for you to say anything now. I know." He glanced over, winked. The accompanying smile was smug.

"What is it that you think you know?"

"You want to invite me in for a drink."

"I want to—"

He cut her off with a *tsking* sound. "But I must refuse."

The hotel was just ahead. Its sign lit up like a beacon.

"You're saying no?" Forget that Darcie hadn't asked or, for that matter, having a drink with him wasn't what had caused her to smile in the first place.

"I was, but all right. One drink. Since you insist."

Nick winked again and turned the car to the right. Just that quickly, he was pulling into the valet parking lane at the front entrance.

"You're something else," she murmured with a shake of her head.

"I will take that as a compliment."

Inside the hotel, he steered her to the lounge. At her questioning glance, he said, "I will not claim to be a saint. A drink in your room poses too much temptation. And we have not yet defined our expectations of our hypothetical fling. Let us move slowly."

"Take our time."

"Drive ourselves insane," it sounded like he said.

So they had a drink in the lounge. Afterward, Nick not only walked her to the elevator, but he also insisted on accompanying her all the way to her room.

"I am not coming in," he assured her when the doors of the elevator slid open on her floor.

"Testing your restraint?" she teased.

He snorted, and it was her restraint that was on the line when he told her, "I want to picture where you will be sleeping tonight."

She opened the door and switched on the light. The room was small with just enough space to accommodate a double bed, dresser, writing desk and television. Housekeeping had been by, so the duvet was turned down, the pillows freshly plumped. A foil-wrapped square of chocolate sat in the center of the one closest to the door.

It wasn't the treat that had her mouth watering.

Darcie's gaze cut to Nick. He was studying her as well, his expression seductive. She had to remind herself that it wouldn't be wise to hop into bed with a man she barely knew, even if what little she did know about him she found very appealing.

"I must go." His tone was brusque.

"Yes."

He gave her a quick kiss on the forehead, pushed her inside and shut the door himself.

"Engage the security chain," she heard him order from the hallway.

With their talk about flings and expectations swirling in her head, it was well after two before Darcie finally fell asleep.

The next day, as promised, she and Nick visited the Temple of Zeus and then Hadrian's Arch. It was a small consolation that he appeared as ill-rested as she was. She had her guidebook out and was reading about how the arch, which was built in 131 AD, had marked the boundary between ancient Athens and the new Roman city of Hadrian, when her cell phone rang.

Thinking it might be Tad, she considered ignoring it, but when she saw that it was Stavros, she flashed Nick an apologetic smile.

"I need to take this."

"I will be just there." He pointed to a nearby street vendor's cart and headed off. Darcie unabashedly enjoyed the view as he walked away. She was smiling when she answered. By the time the call ended five minutes later, however, she was fuming and feeling dejected. It didn't come as a surprise that Stavros would not refund her money. Still, she'd hoped.... She went to join Nick.

"I took a chance that you would like chocolate." He handed her an ice cream cone.

"Gee, big risk," she teased. "Where's yours?"

"Ice cream will melt quickly in this heat. I thought we could share." With that, he ran his tongue over the top scoop, all while keeping his gaze on her.

When Nick said things like that, when he looked at Darcie the way he was looking at her right now... She'd never felt like this. Ever. So wound up. So wanted. Wouldn't it just figure that she would be leaving soon?

"It is your turn now." Nick nodded to the ice cream.

Unfortunately, when she went to lick the ice cream, the

top scoop fell off the cone. It plopped on the pavement between their feet.

"The story of my life," she muttered, closing her eyes.
She wanted to scream, cry. She settled for sighing.

"It is only ice cream. There is no need to be so upset."

She opened her eyes. "It's not just the ice cream."

His expression sobered. "The phone call, has something
happened? Your family?"

"All fine as far as I know. That was Stavros. He finally
got around to returning my call."

"And?"

"Well, he was very apologetic when I asked for a refund,
but..." Her shoulders lifted. "He did offer to personally
drive me to several of the locations on my itinerary, but I
declined. He didn't exactly sound sober."

Nick threw the empty ice cream cone into a nearby waste
container and plucked his cell phone from his back pocket.
"I will call him. I will make him see reason."

"Thank you, but no." She placed a hand over his. "You've
already left messages on my behalf. Besides, you said it
yourself that first day. He doesn't have the money to refund."

"What will you do now?"

"I can't stay the full two weeks." Even if she wanted to—
and oh, yeah, she really wanted to—she couldn't afford it.
As it was, her three nights in Athens were going to set her
back half a week's pay.

"How long?"

"Another couple of days." And even that was going to
stretch her financial limit. It would be worth eating mac
and cheese for a month, though, if it meant spending more
time with Nick.

"But you cannot leave so soon. You have barely seen
any of the sights. You have barely been outside of Athens."

"Believe me, I wish I could afford to continue my vacation, but I can't."

"If you had a place to stay, one that would cost you nothing, would you postpone your return to the States?" he asked slowly.

"What do you mean *if* I had a place to stay that would not cost me anything?"

"I know of such a place, a house that is not far from where we had dinner last night."

"A house?" He had to be joking. A house near the harbor that would not cost her a dime? Her tone light, she asked, "Does it boast the same spectacular view as the restaurant?"

"The view is even better."

"You're serious."

"I am. Do you want to see it?"

"I…"

He took her hand and started toward where he had parked the car. "I will take that as a yes."

Darcie expected the house to be nice. Nick didn't strike her as the sort of man who would recommend anything even remotely substandard. Nor had he exaggerated about the view. The house was farther up the hillside than the restaurant and its windows were placed to make the most of the stunning scenery.

The foyer opened into what she assumed was the main living space. It was spacious, well-appointed.

"Is this really a rental property?"

He didn't answer. Instead, he pointed toward an arched doorway across the room.

"The kitchen is through here," he said.

The home's kitchen was bigger than the one Darcie had glimpsed at Nick's grandmother's house. Even though it was equipped with state-of-the-art appliances, it appeared less used. The stainless steel pots and pans that dangled from the rack over the butcher-block island showed little sign of wear, and there was not so much as a grease splatter on the tiles on the wall behind the cook top. That seemed odd and she said as much to Nick.

He shrugged. "Some people prefer to eat out."

They returned to the living room. She glanced around again. The furnishings were modern and leaned toward masculine with their no-frill lines and muted colors. The massive plasma-screen television would appeal to a man, too. And all of the magazines spread out over the coffee table were geared toward sports and the automobile enthusiast.

"The bedrooms are upstairs," Nick said.

He was three treads up when Darcie's words stopped him. "That's all right. I think I've seen enough."

He turned on a frown. "It is not to your liking."

"Oh, I like it. How can I not? This home is gorgeous." She folded her arms. "It's also no rental. It's yours, Nick."

At least he didn't insult her intelligence by trying to deny it. "I am so rarely here that I could rent it out. In fact, my accountant has suggested I do just that."

Oh, she didn't doubt that. The location was prime, the view stunning, its amenities and furnishings were top-of-the-line. He could lease it by the week or even by the month. It would fetch an outrageous sum.

"You could, but you don't. You're making an exception for me. And my stay would be complimentary."

He dipped his chin. "Yes."

"But there's a price, right?"

She wanted to be irate, maybe even insulted. She was having a hard time getting past flattered and turned on. And that was before he smiled. Heat shimmied up her spine like a brush fire out of control.

"I assure you, it is not what you are thinking."

Arms still crossed, for self-preservation more so than out of pique, she asked, "And what is it that I'm thinking, Nick?"

"That I am trying to take advantage of both you and your current situation."

"Are you?"

"As tempting as I find that, I am a man with scruples, remember? You said so yourself."

"So, what you are saying then, is that if I agree to stay here you would be sleeping on the couch."

His laughter was sharp. "I have scruples, Darcie. But I will not claim to be a saint. If I were to spend the night under the same roof as you, sleeping on the couch would not be an option for either of us."

A disturbingly erotic image of the pair of them—sweaty, sated and tangled up in bedsheets—swirled through her mind. She swallowed hard and managed to say, "Then what do you have in mind?"

He took a step toward her, and even though he was still more than arm's length away, her body began to hum like the plucked strings of a harp.

"I will stay with my family. My mother will be glad for the intrusion. She complains that she does not see me enough when I am in Athens." He took another step forward. "You would have this entire place to yourself. How does that sound?"

Lonely. "Lovely."

"Is that yes, then?"

Darcie gave herself a mental shake. "Nick, your offer is very generous, a little too generous for me to accept."

"I am only repaying your kindness. You did me a favor," he persisted.

"Repayment wasn't necessary. I enjoyed dinner with your family. Besides, you have taken me sightseeing and out to dinner last night. You have more than repaid any debt you feel you owe me."

"Perhaps you will consider staying here in lieu of payment for a job?"

That caught her interest. "What sort of job?"

"You are a trained journalist, yes?"

"I'm a fact-checker."

"You *were* a fact-checker. Regardless, you are a journalist and, most importantly, you know an astonishing amount about vintage automobiles."

"I do," she agreed, still unable to figure out where this was heading.

"In exchange for writing background information for my auction catalog, a service for which I currently pay someone in New York, you can stay in my home for the remainder of your vacation and I will continue to act as your tour guide. We may not be able to hit all of the sites on your original itinerary, but we should be able to manage many of them."

Darcie ran her tongue around her teeth. What he was proposing sounded reasonable. It sounded fair. And, God knew, she didn't want to cut her trip short and fly home to the mess that awaited her. There was so much more she wanted to see and experience in Greece.

And then there was Nick...

"Um, the person who usually does this sort of thing for you, will they be out of work if I agree?"

Nick shook his head. "I have no one on my payroll, if that is what you mean. I contract with a couple of freelance writers in Manhattan whenever the need arises. In this case, I simply would be contracting with you instead."

"And my payment would be free lodgings here."

"And sightseeing. You will have a car at your disposal, should you need one. And I am happy to accompany you."

The smile that spread across his face caused heat to curl

in her belly. As much as she wanted to agree right then and there, Darcie hesitated. "That seems like such an imposition. I can't help but feel like I'm getting the better end of the deal."

"Hmm," Nick murmured thoughtfully as he closed the distance between them. His hands found Darcie's waist and he said, "Then perhaps I should apply conditions."

"Oh? What might those be?" she asked, and gave herself a mental high five for not hyperventilating on the spot. Indeed, for someone who had already confessed to being unsophisticated when it came to matters such as this, Darcie thought she sounded downright blasé.

"You will have to accompany me on my business trips. I have four lined up between now and the day you are to return home." He leaned in after saying so. She felt his lips brush the curve of her neck. "We can combine my business with your pleasure."

"I—I suppose I could fit those into my schedule." She tipped her head to the side, giving him greater access to her neck. While he took advantage of that, she closed her eyes and murmured, "Anything else?"

"You will help me research the vehicles in question. I usually do this on my own, but I would appreciate your insight." His breath tickled her ear.

"Mmm. 'Kay. I have no problem with that."

"No?" He kissed her cheek.

"None whatsoever."

"Good."

"It is good." Bordering on incredible, she decided, as his hands moved up her sides and his thumbs brushed the underside of her breasts.

"So, that is yes?" His voice was low, strained. "You will stay?"

Darcie wrapped her arms around his neck and kissed him. "I'll stay, Nick."

CHAPTER SEVEN

"WE HAD BETTER GO."

Nick made that pronouncement with no small amount of regret. But if he and Darcie stayed in his home much longer, the sparks he was experiencing were bound to ignite into an all-out blaze. And he had just convinced her that he was not, in fact, offering her a place to stay in exchange for a bedmate. He still had no doubt that Darcie and he would move beyond the hypothetical when it came to having a fling, but he'd meant what he said last night—he wanted both of them going into it with open eyes and clear expectations.

That and he couldn't explain exactly why, but he didn't want the flash and burn of spontaneous sex. With Darcie, when it happened, he wanted to take his time. He wanted to make it last, make it count. Something told him she deserved that. So, he collected his keys from the kitchen counter and steered her out the door as quickly as possible. She didn't object.

On the drive back to her hotel, he said, "I will be by tomorrow morning at nine to collect you. We can move your belongings to the house and then spend the afternoon wandering near the seaside, if you would like."

"That sounds fine, but what about work? Do you have a car you need to go see or one that you want me to start researching online?"

Nick shook his head. "I think tomorrow will be a day off for both of us. Work can start the following day."

"Oh, my God! You're moving in with Nick!"

Becky didn't sound as scandalized as she did jealous. And no wonder. After Darcie had sent her friend a photograph she'd snapped of Nick at the Parthenon, Becky had emailed back that she would be on the next flight to Athens if Nick had a friend she could meet who was even half as good-looking.

No friend. Only a brother and he's getting married, Darcie had emailed back. She'd left out all of the nuances to that particular story, not sure what to make of them herself.

Now, she told Becky, "I'm not moving in with Nick. I'm moving into his house."

"You say potato.... Is there really a distinction?"

Darcie couldn't help but laugh. Nor could she help but be grateful that she'd called Becky before calling her family. She could only imagine what her parents were going to make of the latest twist in her trip itinerary. They hadn't exactly been thrilled about her going on her honeymoon solo. Even though she was a grown woman, she knew they worried. She'd promised to check in a few times during her trip. Her conversation with Becky qualified as a test run, so Darcie strove to clear up any misconceptions. She needed to have her story down pat before relaying it to her mom and dad.

"There's a big distinction. Nick will not be there. He is going to stay with his parents."

She went on to explain the rest of the arrangement to Becky—the work she would be doing for Nick in exchange for the free lodgings. By the time she finished, it sounded like a perfectly platonic business deal, especially since she didn't mention the skill with which Nick kissed or the way she responded to those kisses. No sense pouring kerosene on a fire that was already burning cheerfully all on its own.

"So, it's a business arrangement," Becky said slowly.

"Exactly. Who knows? Nick says he uses freelancers to put together his auction booklets. Maybe I'll be able to snag some of that work when I get home, too. It's not exactly full-length feature writing, but it's a start. I can get my feet wet, begin collecting clips."

"You want to write again?"

Darcie had never stopped *wanting* to write, but as a practical matter, while working full-time as a fact-checker, she hadn't had the wherewithal to seek out freelance opportunities. Besides, Tad had not been encouraging. A journalism career, especially one that eventually might take her to New York, wasn't in the cards for his future wife.

"My life is in chaos anyway. Why not try new things? You know, take some chances."

"Oh, you won't get any argument from me. I always felt you gave up on your dream job much too easily. That's another reason I never liked Tad. He wasn't supportive when it came to your goals. It was all about him. His happiness. His career. His mother," she added drolly. "I'm glad to see your backbone returning."

"Greece has been good for me," Darcie replied. "A new start."

"Yes, and a hot man who treats you like a goddess doesn't hurt, either."

They both laughed, but Darcie knew there was some truth to her friend's words. In the short time she'd known Nick, she had started to feel more confident, more desirable, more in control of her future. Maybe those changes would have occurred regardless once she'd called off her engagement. Still, she credited Nick for accelerating the process.

But did that mean she could handle a no-emotional-strings-attached fling with him? Darcie didn't know. Sure, she flirted a good game, but she'd also confessed her unworldliness to Nick. She was pretty sure that was what had him holding back.

After Darcie hung up, she called her mom and dad.

Neither of her parents had a problem with her new living arrangements, especially since Darcie left off the part that Nick owned the house where she would be staying. In fact, she left out a lot of details where Nick was concerned, only mentioning that he'd offered her a freelance opportunity.

Like Becky, her father was thrilled that Darcie was returning to writing.

"That's the best news I've had in a long, long time," he told her. The pride she heard in his voice made her eyes sting. He'd never stopped believing in her.

"Thanks, Dad." Since her mother was on the extension, Darcie asked, "And you, Mom? What do you think?"

"I'm happy if you're happy." But her voice didn't hold pride as much as trepidation.

"But?"

"I don't know." Then, apropos of nothing, she said, "Tad stopped by today. He dropped off some wedding gifts from our side of the family that had been mailed to the condo."

Not sure what else to say, Darcie replied, "That was nice of him."

"He also brought a box of miscellaneous things you left behind when you moved out."

"Oh." Again, she was at a loss for words.

"I know you often felt second in line to his mother, but by calling off the wedding, well, I think you've made your point. I think things would be different now if you got back together. He…he really loves you."

Darcie swallowed, wishing it were as simple as that.

Wishing she could want the same suburban life her married sisters had so happily embraced.

"But I don't love him, Mom. Not the way I should if I am going to spend the rest of my life as his wife."

"He said he's been trying to reach you but that you haven't returned any of his calls."

Four on her cell. All of which Darcie had let go to voice mail. "I know. And I will."

"When?"

"When I get back."

"Honey—"

"Mom, please. It's over. You need to accept that and so does Tad. He and I, well, we want different things in life."

"What is it that you want, Darcie?" Her mother's tone had turned impatient. "What is it you *think* you're looking for?"

It was her father who answered. "Stop badgering the girl. She simply wants more than what Tad can offer."

Darcie closed her eyes. Bless her dad. He got it. He understood. Her mother, meanwhile, remained perplexed.

"Are you sure it's not just a case of cold feet?" she asked. "A lot of brides get them. It's natural."

"I'm positive, Mom."

And Darcie was, especially when she thought about Nick and all of the heat the man could generate inside of her with a single, simple smile.

The move to Nick's house the next morning was accomplished easily. Darcie had only the one, forlorn-looking bag after all. She'd still heard nothing from the airline about her missing piece of luggage. With her luck, it would show up in Greece about the time she was to return home. Whatever. She was making do and, now that she didn't have to worry about paying for lodgings, she'd decided she was entitled to make a few more wardrobe purchases. Already Nick had mentioned having dinner again. She couldn't very well keep wearing the same dress. And she was starting to feel a little too touristy outfitted in T-shirts, shorts and sneakers. She might as well hang a camera around her neck and strap on a fanny pack to complete the cliché.

Once they arrived at Nick's house, she stood in the driveway and breathed in the sea-scented air, looking forward to the stroll through town that he promised her. The day was warm, but the breeze kept the temperature from being unpleasant.

That was until they went inside and Nick offered a tempting smile and said, "We never got to the bedrooms yesterday."

They hadn't gotten to a lot of things while in his house the day before, Darcie thought, not sure whether it was relief she felt or something more damning.

Even so, she smiled in return and made a sweeping motion with one hand. "Lead the way."

Three bedrooms opened up off the hallway at the top of the stairs. Each had its own bath. Two of the rooms, including the master, faced the harbor and sported private balconies. The master was large enough to accommodate a small sitting area in addition to a king-sized bed. The chairs were upholstered in a luscious aquamarine, which, when combined with the deep blue duvet cover, mimicked the colors of the harbor. The art on the walls featured nautical themes, although the works themselves were more abstract in nature. Darcie was no connoisseur, but the pictures appeared to be signed originals or numbered prints, all of which were expertly matted and framed.

Nick came up behind her as she gazed out at the harbor. She swore she could feel the heat from his body warming her back even though he stood a respectable distance away.

"This is a very, um, restful view," she said.

"You would think so." Dry humor tinged his voice. "Right now, I am feeling very restless, especially when I think of you sleeping in my bed."

"About that." She cleared her throat and turned. "I think I will take one of your guestrooms."

"Are you sure? I spared no expense on that mattress. I think you would be more comfortable in here."

She didn't agree. Indeed, she had a feeling that she would toss and turn all night on the mattress in question, tortured by detailed fantasies and the lingering scent of his cologne. She wasn't quite ready to slip into Nick's bed—alone or otherwise.

Darcie chose the guestroom next door. It offered the same stunning view as the master and could hardly be considered small, even if it only had one chair rather than an actual sitting area. If she wanted to sit at all up here, she would do it on the balcony in one of the cushioned chaises.

It only took her a few minutes to unpack her clothes and toiletries, and then she met Nick downstairs, where he showed her around his home office. Like the rest of the house, the furnishings were modern with clean lines. The wooden desk was stained a deep brown. The bookshelves just behind it were glass and metal. Every electronic gadget one could wish for—tablet, laptop, digital printer and copier—would be at her disposal.

He showed her how to log on to the internet using his laptop, as well as how to access her own email account. With a few clicks of the mouse, he also brought up a raft of research sites that he used to locate collectible cars and determine their value. Given her current job, she was familiar with several of them. Then he opened a file on the laptop and pulled up a catalog from a previous auction at his warehouse just outside Manhattan. It had been created using software Darcie knew well. In addition to color photographs of the automobiles and the prices they were likely to bring at auction, the catalog included several paragraphs describing the vehicles.

Nick tapped his index finger against the screen. "This is the sort of thing I will need you to write for me. Facts tend to be bland. Bland does not generate interest, let alone bids. People need to be persuaded to part with their money, especially in such vast sums. The catalogs are sent out in advance and help generate not only interest, but excitement."

She grinned. She knew where he was heading. "Trust me. The facts won't be bland or boring when I get done with them. I'll make those cars sound so sexy and irresistible that even you will be tempted to bid on them when they come up for auction."

"That is exactly what I was hoping to hear."

Darcie's gaze fell on a framed picture of a younger Nick standing with another man in front of a race car. His uncle, she surmised, recalling their conversation from the day they met. This was the man who had kick-started Nick's passion for cars and, ultimately, set into motion his career.

"Does your uncle still race?"

"No. He is retired. But racing is in his blood. He sponsors other drivers now." Nick pointed to the photograph. "He still owns that car. He won a Grand Prix with it. He retired not long afterward and the car retired with him. He said he couldn't part with it."

"Is it difficult?" she asked.

"Is what difficult?"

"Parting with the cars that you like?" She sent him a grin. "It's obvious that you have a weakness for a finely engineered automobile."

"I do, but they are not my only weakness." His gaze was on her mouth.

"Nick," she said pointedly.

"What were we talking about again?" he asked.

"Cars. Selling them. Even the ones you would like to keep for yourself."

"Ah. Yes. I remember now." He shook his head and shrugged. "I enjoy the automobiles while they are in my possession. That is enough." His gaze was on her mouth again. "I do not need to own something to enjoy it. Not everything is meant to last."

His words, the intensity of his gaze, caused a shiver to run up her spine. A vacation fling was the perfect example. Meant to be enjoyed. Meant to end. Darcie found the thought unsettling, but she shouldn't have. If it was permanence she sought, she should have stayed with Tad. He was the man who'd offered for her hand. No, Darcie had other ambitions, newly revived ones that were just begging to be explored, exploited. Nick was giving her that chance. Anything else that transpired between them came without strings.

"Well, it had better be enough, because you'll never see them again once I give them a write-up."

He stroked the hair back from her face. Where a moment ago his expression had been intense, it was thoughtful now. "I heard it said once that writers are artists who paint pictures with words. So, you are an artist, Darcie Hayes."

How long had it been since she'd seen herself that way? Since she'd last dared to see herself that way? Confidence—new and heady—swelled inside her.

"Thank you."

"I do not want your gratitude."

"But you have it," she argued. He couldn't possibly know what he'd done by giving her this opportunity. To lighten the moment, however, she rubbed her hands together and said, "I can't wait to get started."

"So eager." He took her hands in his. "But tomorrow

will be soon enough. Today we will enjoy ourselves. Are you hungry?"

"Starving. I skipped breakfast," she admitted.

"That is no good. You should never deny yourself."

The man had a point, Darcie thought. She had denied herself a lot the past several years—not food, but other things that, in some ways, were every bit as vital to her well-being. He still had her hands in his. He turned one over, brought it to his mouth for a kiss. A moan escaped. Who knew the palm was an erogenous zone?

Nick leaned toward her, their mouths met. Not far away was a bedroom, one with a mattress for whose quality he had already vouched. She edged back on a sigh.

"Lunch?"

He rested his forehead against hers. "I thought we had just established that you should not deny yourself."

"You're tempting me."

"I should hope so." His laughter was gruff as he stepped back. "But you are not ready and I promised that whatever happened between us would occur naturally and be mutually agreeable. The timing is not right. You need more romance, I think."

She swallowed, liking the sound of that. "So, lunch?"

He swept a hand toward the door. "After you."

They ate near the harbor, in a small bistro that Nick frequented when he was in town. The owner was a big man with craggy features and a booming laugh. He knew Nick by sight if not by name, so he smiled in welcome when they entered.

Lunch was a busy time, but since it was later in the afternoon, the crowd already had thinned. They took a table near the back of the small restaurant.

"Do you know everyone in Greece?" Darcie asked once they were seated.

"No, but I make it a point to get to know the people I like." He reached for her hand. "Take you, for example. I find myself wanting to know everything there is to know."

He said it lightly, but he meant it. He hadn't felt this interested in anything besides automobiles in a very long time. But there was no denying he was curious about Darcie, not to mention intensely curious about the man to whom she so recently had been engaged.

"You want to hear the story of my life?" she asked on a laugh.

"Yes. I believe you promised to tell it to me that first day."

"You already know I'm a magnet for disaster and cursed with bad luck. The rest, I'm afraid, is rather boring."

"I will be the judge."

"All right. But you go first." When he blinked in surprise, she added, "It goes both ways, you know. I have a lot of questions I wouldn't mind having answered, too."

"So, we should satisfy each other's curiosity. Is that what you are saying?"

"It's only fair."

"Ask then."

Nick knew Darcie had chickened out when she inquired, "What's your favorite color?"

"Red. My turn." And he went for the jugular. "How long did you know your former fiancé?"

"Too long."

"That is not an answer," he chastised.

"Get comfortable then," she teased. "And, don't worry. I'll wake you up if you fall asleep."

The server came for their order. When they were alone again, Nick motioned with his hand. "Go on. I am wide-awake and promise to stay that way. For the record, I am always interested in what you have to say."

Darcie swallowed. While it was a bit disconcerting to have Nick's full attention focused on her, she liked that about him. He didn't just pretend to listen to her. He really did, making it impossible to hide behind her usual flippant replies and offhand remarks. Who knew, maybe telling him about Tad would be cathartic rather than merely embarrassing. Maybe it would make it clear not only to Nick, but also to herself that the past was behind her and it was time to grab the present by the horns.

"Well, I met Tad during my senior year of college. I had a really bad throat infection and went to the clinic on campus to get it checked out. He was a first-year intern and working that afternoon."

"He was your doctor? Kinky." Nick arched his eyebrows.

"No! Well, I guess technically he was for that one visit, but I kept my clothes on. Remember, tonsils." She pointed to her throat. "They're up here."

"I am well-versed in a woman's anatomy."

"I'm sure you are." She cleared her throat. "Anyway, the two of us got to chatting. My tonsils were enlarged, something that happened quite often. He thought they might need to come out."

"You talked about enlarged tonsils and somehow still wound up going on a date?"

Darcie pulled a face. "It must have seemed romantic at the time."

"If you say so. Go on."

"There's not much more to tell. Tad and I started dating and then, six years ago, he proposed."

Nick's eyes widened at that. "The two of you were engaged for six years? Did you live together the entire time?"

"No. I moved in once he agreed to a wedding date. That

was two years ago. Tad didn't want to get married until he was done with his residency and ready to start a practice of his own. Evelyn thought it would be too distracting."

"His mother."

Darcie frowned. "I tried to be understanding. She's a widow and Tad is her only child. He's all the family she has. But the closer our wedding came, the clingier and more demanding of Tad's time she became."

"What did your family think of him?"

"Ah-ah-ah. It's my turn to ask a question."

He bowed his head.

"Do you...like scary movies?"

Nick stashed his grin. She'd chickened out again. "No. What did your family think of Tad?"

She exhaled, clearly irritated. "My sisters liked him. I think they liked the idea of me being engaged and heading toward the altar even more than they liked Tad. My mom is still hoping this is just a case of cold feet. Tad was very sweet to her, always full of compliments."

"And your father?"

She rubbed her chin. "Dad never really said anything one way or another while Tad and I were engaged, but I get the feeling he isn't all that upset I called it off, even if he's on the hook for a lot of nonrefundable deposits now."

"Let me guess, you gave up pursuing your career around the time you and Tad got engaged? Your father did not like Tad because he wanted you to follow your dream, and he knew you would give up on it forever if you married someone like Tad. You had taken a job checking facts rather than writing pieces whose facts other people would check for you."

It made sense to him now how she wound up in a career for which she had no passion.

"That about sums it up," she said.

"And so you ended things."

"One week before 'I do.'" Both her tone and her expression were grim. "Not exactly my classiest moment."

"Better one week before than one week after."

"I guess that's one way to look at it." The server returned with their drinks. "My turn again."

"All right."

He figured she would wimp out again. So, he nearly spit out the mouthful of sparkling water when she said, "What are your feelings for Selene?"

"I have no feelings for her. She is marrying my brother. End of story."

"Okay." Darcie accepted the cryptic answer with a nod. Then she hit him with both barrels by asking, "What are your feelings for your brother?"

"I miss him," Nick replied honestly, surprising himself.

CHAPTER EIGHT

NICK WOKE IN his boyhood bedroom to the smell of fresh bread—the crusty variety that his mother and grandmother routinely made in an outdoor wood-burning oven that straddled the property line between their two houses. The scent wafted through the open window, drawing him upright.

He'd spent the past four nights under his parents' roof after spending his days with Darcie. As promised, they divided their time between sightseeing and work. He was enjoying both and he thought she was, too.

Already, she'd presented him with research on three vehicles, including estimated values for the vehicles based on what similar models had brought at recent auctions. She was thorough, conscientious and professional, and damn if he didn't find that all very sexy.

He wanted her. Had since that first glance in the airport. But he was treading carefully for reasons that he couldn't quite explain, since nothing about their relationship called for permanence. Darcie was newly single, finding her way, spreading her wings. He admired her for that. She wouldn't be looking to settle down so soon again. Especially with a man who lived so far away. Besides, Nick had no personal capital to invest in a relationship. He hadn't since Selene.

So why was he finding the idea of sleeping with Darcie and then saying goodbye less appealing by the day?

They were taking things slowly, more slowly than he'd ever moved with a woman. Nick supposed Darcie's candor where her ex-fiancé was concerned was among the reasons he was treading with care. She had been marginalized, made to feel unimportant by the man who was supposed to love her. Recalling the conversation at the restaurant, Nick could admit she had been painfully honest about her past relationship, whereas he had not divulged much at all when it came to Selene. The only secret he'd shared was that he missed his brother.

Admittedly, the revelation had come as a surprise to Nick. But it still didn't come close to all of the soul-baring Darcie had done, and he regretted that.

Meanwhile, he and Darcie continued to play it safe, flirting with abandon, even as they tiptoed around the land mines of their pasts. Safe. Sure. As long as he didn't recall how heated their flirtation turned at times.

On a groan, he got up and took a shower—the cold variety—before wandering to the kitchen. He came up short when he saw Pieter seated at the table. Nick had managed to avoid him since that evening at Yiayia's.

"What are you doing here?"

"Do I need a reason to visit our parents?" Pieter shot back. "Besides, the better question is what are you doing sleeping here when you have a bed elsewhere?"

"It's occupied at the moment."

Pieter smiled. "Precisely my point."

"Is there more coffee?"

Nick motioned to the *briki.* His mother had been brewing coffee in the traditional, long-handled pot for more than three decades. He had a *briki* at his house, too. The copper pot was as bright and shiny as the day it was made since it never saw any use. The same could be said for his electric coffeemaker—both the one here and the one back in New

York. What did it say about him, Nick wondered, that he owned a house and an apartment, but neither felt like home?

In answer to his question, Pieter got up and poured the last of the coffee into a demitasse cup and handed it to Nick.

"Thank you," he said stiffly. Although he was tempted to leave, he took the chair opposite his brother.

"It looks like you had a rough night." Pieter didn't bother to hide his grin.

Until just a few years ago, such good-natured teasing between the brothers had been common. Nick didn't want to miss it. He didn't want to miss Pieter. But, just as he'd admitted to Darcie, he did. He sipped the coffee. It was strong and very sweet. That was how their mother always made it, but it did little to improve his sour mood.

Head bent over his cup, he grumbled, "I don't remember that mattress being quite so lumpy."

The mattress wasn't why he'd slept so poorly, though, and they both knew it.

"I never realized how chivalrous you were. Yiayia even commented on it."

Nick grunted and took another sip of coffee.

"She is sure this is a sign."

"Yiayia and her signs," Nick mumbled. "Everything is a sign to her."

"But is she right in this case?" Pieter set his cup back on its saucer. He was no longer grinning when he asked, "Have you found someone…special?"

Nick stared into his coffee. "Darcie is special."

"Is it serious?"

"It is…complicated," Nick replied truthfully, uncomfortably.

The evasive answer had his brother nodding. "Love is always complicated."

"And you would know!" Nick challenged.

Pieter didn't take the bait. Instead, he replied, "I am happy for you. All of us are. Mama and Yiayia can talk of nothing else."

That should have pleased Nick. It was why he had introduced Darcie to them, after all. With his supposed girlfriend as the topic of their conversations until the wedding, he would no longer have to worry about them trying to set him up. But he felt uneasy.

"What are they saying about Darcie?" he asked.

"It's not so much what they are saying about her, although obviously they like her. It's more the effect Darcie has had on you. You seem like your old self again. Mama and Yiayia are happy you have found someone. As am I."

Emotions crowded in. Nick pushed away all but anger. Arching an eyebrow, he said sarcastically, "So we can be one big happy family again? Do you really think that possible, Pieter?"

His brother swallowed. "It is what I hope, what I want."

"And you get whatever you want. Or you take it, as the case may be."

Pieter looked gut-punched. "You are not being fair."

"Fairness, brother? Really?" His voice rose. Nick rose along with it. Palms planted on the tabletop, he demanded, "You want to talk about fairness?"

Pieter was on his feet as well. "You made your choices, Nick. You are the one who decided to leave Greece, to set up a business in New York, far away from family. Far away from Selene."

"And you were here to offer comfort and company," he added caustically.

But Pieter didn't back down. "You chased *your* dream without bothering to ask her what she wanted. You just expected that she would drop everything, leave everyone behind and follow you."

Nick's conscience stung. Was that what he'd done? Darcie came to mind. She'd sacrificed her dream of feature writing for her fiancé, settling for a fact-checking job at a small trade publication instead. Ultimately, what she'd given up had only fed her dissatisfaction and resentment. Had Nick done the same thing to Selene? If she had followed him to New York, would their relationship have survived?

Because he did not care for the face staring back at him from the mirror in his mind, his tone was harsh when he told his brother, "That is not what I expected, dammit!"

"Then what?" Pieter challenged. "What did you expect?"

Darcie, Selene—both women were forgotten now. Nick saw only Pieter, his brother and, at one time, his very best friend.

"I did not expect you to betray me!" He pounded his fist on the tabletop with enough force to rattle their coffee cups. There it was, the crux of the matter. The one big stumbling block Nick could not surmount, regardless of the number of times he'd tried. "While I was gone, I asked you to look after Selene for me. I knew she would be lonely. I did not think—"

Pieter's fists were clenched at his sides. "How many times must I tell you that is not how it happened? Selene and I did not betray you!"

The brothers glared at one another across the table.

"I do not care about Selene." And it was true, Nick realized. His feelings for his childhood sweetheart were over. "But you! My own brother. I *trusted* you."

"I did nothing to betray you or your trust. God knows! I fought the attraction I felt for her, and I felt it since we were all teenagers. Do you know what it was like to have her choose you?"

Nick blinked. He hadn't known. Had not even suspected. Would he have cared if he had? His anger now, however, was greater than any concern he felt for Pieter's feelings in the past. "So, you got even? Is that it?"

"No." The fight had gone out of his brother. Pieter slumped down in his seat. His voice was quiet, but his words were no less potent when he said, "I love her, I have always loved her, but I never imagined…I never dared to hope… You have to believe me that it was long after the two of you had parted ways that anything developed between us. Even so, we both tried to deny it." Pieter shoved a hand through his hair, his eyes bright with pain, frustration and resignation when he added, "Some things cannot be denied."

The door opened and their mother rushed into the kitchen from the yard. Her face was flushed, her expression one of worry.

"What on earth has happened? Your raised voices can be heard all the way to the coast!"

"Nothing happened," Nick told her, feeling more shaken than he wanted to admit. He crossed to the sink and tossed the remainder of his coffee down the drain.

As he stalked from the room, he heard Pieter say wearily, "He cannot forgive me."

Darcie was at the computer in Nick's home office working on some research when she heard a car pull up the driveway. Her mouth curved into a smile as she recognized the purr of the Jag's powerful motor. Then she glanced at the clock, puzzled. He was almost two hours early for their drive to Trikala. They had an afternoon meeting with a potential buyer for the Porsche he'd been driving the day they met.

Was that really only a week ago? It was hard to believe given all that had occurred since then. Indeed, over the past two weeks Darcie's entire life had been turned upside down. She'd gone from being an uncertain and disenchanted bride-to-be to a single woman who was determined to hammer out a new future for herself. And having a fine time doing it, thanks to Nick.

Her heart skipped a beat when she heard the door open. She turned, intending to tease him about being so eager, but her own smile died upon seeing his dire expression.

"Are you ready to leave?" he asked.

"I, um…" She glanced back at the computer, where she had several files open. "Can you give me another fifteen minutes? I just need to check a couple more things and print this out."

He nodded. "I will be on the terrace."

When she finished, she joined him there. He was so pre-occupied that he didn't even hear her approach. When she laid a hand on his shoulder, he turned abruptly, almost as if he expected to find someone else standing there.

"Nick, is everything all right?"

"Yes. Of course." But his eyes remained dark and fath-omless and at odds with the smile that turned up the corners of his mouth. "I am looking forward to our trip."

After Trikala, they were going to continue on to Me-teora, where they would stay the night in a hotel. Even though Darcie had not asked him to, Nick had booked separate rooms for them, and of course he had insisted on paying for both. First thing in the morning, the plan was to tour a couple of Meteora's remaining six Greek Or-thodox monasteries that were built atop rocky sandstone towers. Then the two of them would head back to Athens.

She had been looking forward to the trip as well. But now…?

"What's wrong?" She laid a hand on his arm. "And please don't tell me 'nothing.' I want to help."

"I thank you for your concern. But you cannot help me."

"Nick," she pleaded.

"I had an argument with my brother this morning." He

waved one hand in dismissal. Even so, Darcie's stomach took a tumble.

"Selene?" she suggested.

Nick's gaze returned to the sea. In profile, Darcie watched his jaw clench. "It is an old wound, but it has not healed properly." He sighed wearily then. "I do not know if it ever will."

"Sometimes talking to a neutral third party helps. I've been told I'm a good listener." When he turned, she offered an encouraging smile. Even so, it was a full minute before Nick said anything.

"I have been so angry. And I have felt entitled to that anger."

"But now?"

He swallowed and shoved a hand through his hair, leaving it as messy as his emotions. The expletive that followed—and she didn't doubt it was an expletive—was spoken in Greek.

"Why don't you tell me what happened between you and Selene?" Maybe by taking a step back in time, he would be able to move forward.

"Selene and I had been seeing one another for a couple of years when I went to New York for the first time. I had saved up some money, and my uncle had a contact in the United States. I planned to attend a few auctions, gain some understanding of the business and return to Athens to build my company here."

"But you stayed."

"Not at first, but eventually. The market for classic automobiles is so much larger in America. It made sense!" He was less emphatic when he added, "Selene did not see it that way."

"Were the two of you engaged at the time?"

He shook his head. "I never proposed, but I thought we had an understanding."

"And moving to another country, was that part of the understanding?"

He frowned. "She did not want to leave Athens."

"Of course not. Everything familiar to her is here," Darcie said. "It was a lot to ask."

"I know." He pinched his eyes closed. "We argued about it more than once, each trying to sway the other. I tried to find a solution. The best I could manage was a compromise. I came back to Greece as often as I could." He lifted his shoulders in a shrug.

"Did she ever come to New York?"

"Once. It was right after I took an apartment there. As much as I love Manhattan, that is how much she hated it. Still, I told myself that eventually…" His words trailed off and he shook his head.

"How long have Pieter and Selene been together?"

"Officially, they have been engaged for the past year. They dated for a year before that. Unofficially? I do not want to know, although they have both assured me repeatedly that I was long out of the picture when they started seeing one another."

"You don't believe them?"

"I am not sure what I believe." He sighed heavily.

Darcie glanced out at the harbor. The water was calm now, as was Nick, but when storms blew in, she imagined that the surface would turn choppy and become dotted with whitecaps that could wrest a small boat from its moorings and swamp it. That must have been how Nick had felt when he'd returned to Athens to find his brother courting Selene.

"You feel betrayed."

"Pieter and I are—were—more than brothers. There is barely a year between our births. We did everything together. We were always the best of friends. There was no one I trusted more."

"That must make this situation all the more difficult," she said softly and rested a hand on his arm. "You lost your best friend and…and the woman you loved."

"Did I?" Nick uttered the question softly. His dark eyes were full of pain when he added, "Did I truly love her? Did Tad love you? Is that how love works?"

Darcie frowned. "I'm afraid I don't understand what you mean."

"Real love would not take more than it gave. It would not be selfish," Nick said. Darcie thought of the Bible verse from First Corinthians that she'd asked one of her brothers-in-law to read at her wedding. *Love is patient. Love is kind… it is not self-seeking….* She always felt it underscored love's many good qualities.

"But Tad was selfish with you. From what you have told me, he put himself, his needs and his wants first. And I was that way with Selene. I knew from the beginning that she did not want to move to America. I knew that she wanted a life here, a life like the one she now will have with Pieter."

"Are you sorry?" Darcie swallowed.

"I hurt her. Yes, for that I am very sorry."

But that wasn't what Darcie meant, so she tried again. "Knowing everything that you know, do you…do you wish you had made a different set of choices?"

"I cannot rewrite history."

"Tad wants to." She hadn't meant to say that.

"What do you mean?"

"Nothing."

"Darcie," he pleaded.

"He's left several messages on my cell." She shrugged.

"And?"

"There is no *and*. I'm just saying that even if we cannot

rewrite history that doesn't mean we don't have regrets. So, do you?" She returned to her original question, afraid of what the answer might be.

"No."

But his expression remained so pained that she wondered. Could he still love Selene? The possibility left her uncomfortable, but why? She had no claim on Nick. No right to expect exclusivity when it came to his affection. They hadn't slept together, even if Darcie could admit that was the direction they were heading, albeit at a slow and measured pace. And when they did, she knew it would be casual. Mind-blowing, but casual. So why did it matter?

Because Darcie feared she was trading one emotionally unavailable man for another.

CHAPTER NINE

NICK SWAPPED HIS Jag for the 1963 Porsche 356 that was parked in the garage and they were on their way. If all went as planned in Trikala, his client would buy the Porsche and they would drive away in a 1956 Austin-Healey roadster that, depending on its condition, would knock off most of the Porsche's asking price. The Austin-Healey, meanwhile, would be featured in Nick's next auction.

It took them just over three hours to make the trip to Trikala. Nick remained preoccupied and introspective the entire way, even though Darcie tried to draw him out in conversation. It was a relief when they finally arrived at their destination, but they were more than two hours early for their meeting.

"We can take a walk through Trikala's scenic old town, if you would like?" Nick said.

Since it would kill some time and might just help shake him from his mood, she readily agreed.

Fifteen minutes into their stroll, she was fanning herself. The heat was stifling and the light breeze's effect on it negligible. They stopped at a café and he bought her *Kliafa*, a refreshing orange drink that was perfect given the day's heat.

After taking a sip, she gravitated to the window of a nearby shop. She couldn't help herself. Shoes were on display and all but calling her name.

"Would you like to go inside?" Nick asked. He was smiling, the first real smile she'd seen all day.

"You don't know what you're saying," she warned with mock sternness.

"Pardon?"

"No man in his right mind encourages a woman to shop."

He took her drink and sipped it straight from the straw. All the while his gaze was on her. "I have a condition."

The simple statement managed to raise gooseflesh on her skin despite the day's heat.

"And that is?"

"Everything that you try on you must model for me."

She glanced back at the shoes. "I'm game."

It was an easy enough deal to keep in a shoe store, but then Nick steered her into a shop two doors down.

"Remember our deal," he said, pointing to a display of lingerie.

"I am *not* trying that on," she said resolutely of the bustier. "But I will try on these." She selected a pair of stone-colored capri pants from one of the racks. "And this."

Nick fingered the soft fabric of the turquoise tunic-style blouse in her hands. "The color will complement your complexion and bring out your eyes."

Darcie tried not to glance at the price tag, which she knew would not complement her bank account. For kicks, she added to the growing selection a white halter dress that made her think of Marilyn Monroe.

"I would really like to see you in this."

Clipped to the hanger he held was a tiny bikini that would leave even more of Darcie exposed than the lingerie.

"Right." She snorted indelicately. "I haven't worn a two-piece swimsuit since I was six years old."

He thrust the hanger into her hands. "Then I would say you are overdue."

"Nick."

"Ah, ah, ah. We had a deal." He nudged her toward the changing room in the back of the store. "Keep in mind that on many European beaches it is perfectly acceptable to go topless."

Laughing, she ducked into the small room. She lined up the hangers, leaving the bikini for last and far from certain she would honor their bargain. The first thing she stepped out in was the white halter dress.

"Ta-da!" In her bare feet, she executed a twirl for him and then posed with one hand on her hip. With the other she primped her hair. "I'm channeling Marilyn Monroe."

"Very sexy. Perhaps the store has an air-conditioning duct you can stand over top of. I would not mind seeing a little more of your legs."

Darcie hiked up the hem of the dress's skirt by a couple of inches to accommodate his wish, but he wasn't satisfied.

"Make no mistake, you have very nice knees. However, I was thinking about your thighs." His smile held a dare.

She glanced around. The shop was busy, but the dressing rooms were at the back. A couple of sale racks helped to shield her from view.

She inched up the dress more slowly this time.

"I will tell you when to stop," Nick said quietly.

"I bet."

The hem was not quite to the middle of her thigh when Nick uttered a gruff, "Enough!"

"You don't want to see any more?"

"Not out in public."

Darcie didn't smile, but she wanted to. The same went for pumping her fists in the air. Eat your heart out, Marilyn, she thought, feeling every bit as desired as the famous sex symbol.

Nick stood. "I'm going to buy another *Kliafa*."

"Right now? I was going to model the bikini next," she teased ruthlessly.

After muttering something she couldn't quite catch, he said, "I will wait for you outside."

So it was that Nick never got the chance to see Darcie wearing a clingy wine-colored dress that an ambitious saleswoman slipped into the changing room along with some sexy satin undergarments that the young woman claimed were essential to ensuring the dress's proper fit.

Darcie had to admit, they definitely smoothed out certain areas while lifting others, which was why she purchased them. As for the bikini, she wasn't sure why she bought it. She didn't need it. Wasn't sure she had the guts to wear it out in public. But she looked good in it. Damned good. A little voice that sounded suspiciously like her friend Becky told her she should buy it.

At the cash register, she wound up charging enough to her credit card to leave her feeling guilty and a little giddy.

"You are flushed," Nick noted as they made their way to the restaurant.

"Yes, well, spending more than I earn in a week has been known to have that effect on me." She chuckled weakly.

Despite their shopping trip, the man they were to meet had not yet arrived when they reached the restaurant. Nick requested a table in a shady part of the patio that offered a lovely view of the Litheos River.

"While we're waiting, why don't you tell me a little about Ari Galanos," Darcie said.

"Ah, Ari." Nick chuckled fondly. "I should warn you, he will flirt shamelessly with you. The man goes through cars almost as quickly as he goes through wives."

"Thanks for the warning." The waiter came by for their beverage order.

"A glass of wine?" Nick asked.

"Why not? I'm not driving."

"You could, you know. If you wished."

"No, no." She shook her head. "With or without a glass of wine, that wouldn't be a good idea."

"The roads can be a little treacherous if one is not familiar with them," he agreed.

"Yes, not to mention the fact that it's been a decade since I last drove a manual transmission." She tilted her head to one side and asked, "Are you familiar with the expression, 'If you can't find 'em, grind 'em'?"

"I am not."

"Well, suffice it to say, that was my motto whenever I was trying to shift from one gear to the next."

"Ah." He grimaced as understanding dawned. And they both wound up chuckling.

"This is nice," Darcie said on a sigh a few minutes later, as she sipped her wine and gazed at the river. "I feel very relaxed."

"That is the point of a vacation, yes? To relax, rejuvenate one's spirit."

She nodded. But they both knew this wasn't a normal vacation for Darcie. The trip had been booked as her honeymoon. After calling off her wedding, she had intended to use it as a getaway, a timeout from her post-breakup reality. Now, it was turning into a job opportunity and so much more.

"Thank you."

"For what?" he asked, surprised.

"For helping me get my life back in order."

"Your gratitude is not necessary. You have done that all on your own."

But she persisted. "No, you had a hand in it, Nick. If not for you, I would be on a plane headed home right now, and going back to a job that I'd talked myself into believing was good enough since it pays the bills."

He reached across the table for her hand, giving it a squeeze. "You sell yourself short, Darcie. You would have reached for your dream again, with or without my help. I gave you a gentle push in the right direction. That is all."

Her smile told Nick she didn't quite believe him. Her gratitude made him uncomfortable. Another man might have used it, exploited it even, to maneuver her into his bed. Nick was too scrupulous for that. He wanted Darcie there, and the waiting was taking its toll, but he did not want her to say yes because she felt she owed him something. He meant it when he told her she would have sought out her dream again on her own, even without his prodding. If her passion for writing was anything like his passion for cars, it wouldn't be denied.

Ari arrived as they were finishing their wine. He ordered a second round of drinks, although this time Nick switched to sparkling water. Not only would he be driving later, but he also preferred to keep a clear head in business. Ari was shrewd and he was used to getting his way.

As predicted, the older man's eyes lit with appreciation when Nick introduced him to Darcie.

Still holding her hand, he said in Greek, "Nick did not mention hiring an assistant. Or is your relationship more personal in nature?"

Smiling, Darcie glanced helplessly at Nick.

"Darcie does not speak Greek," he said. "She is an American."

"I apologize," Ari replied in heavily accented English. "I was asking about your relationship with Nick."

"My re—"

"Darcie is a writer," Nick explained. "I have hired her to prepare feature articles on some of the automobiles that will appear in my next auction brochure. Already she has done some research on your Austin-Healey."

Ari didn't appear convinced. His tone was just shy of condescending when he asked, "What have you managed to learn about my automobile, my dear?"

"Let's see, I know the 1956 model is worth more than other 100M Roadsters." She ran a fingertip around the top of her wineglass as she spoke. "That was the only year they manufactured the performance-enhanced model, which tops out at a speed of one hundred and fifteen miles per hour. The car was marketed to customers who wanted to compete or who just plain liked to go fast, which is why it has a tighter front suspension, added louvers to keep the hood in place at high speeds and a fold-down windshield."

Ari's bushy brows shot up. "Beautiful *and* smart. I apologize."

"Darcie is not to be underestimated," Nick agreed with no small amount of pride. And he knew a moment of panic as he wondered if he had underestimated the impact she was having on his life.

Earlier, she had thanked him for helping her to get her life back in order. For helping her find passion again where it long had been missing. It dawned on Nick that she had returned the favor. He always had enjoyed business. It was his personal life that had been lacking. Oh, he'd dated plenty of women, one or two of them for several months before breaking off the relationship and moving on.

None of those women had affected him the way Darcie was. None had made him envision a future with a family that he'd taken for granted when he was a young man.

The drive from Trikala to their hotel in Meteora would have taken less than half an hour, but Nick wanted to put his newly acquired Austin-Healey through its paces.

"Satisfied with the car?" Darcie asked when traffic finally forced him to slow down.

"I am, yes. Ari has taken good care of her. She runs like a dream." He rubbed the leather seat. "And other than this one small tear in the upholstery, her body is in mint condition, as well."

"Why do men refer to cars with female pronouns? I've never understood that."

"It seems more natural to be riding in a female than a male." Nick grinned. "Maybe it is simply the way we are wired."

"So, you're saying it's in your genes?" Darcie rolled her eyes. "Please."

His grin turned wicked. "A different kind of jeans then."

Darcie crossed her arms over her chest and rolled her eyes a second time, but she looked more amused than exasperated. He wasn't sure how she'd managed it, but over the course of the day, she'd drawn him out of his foul mood. Indeed, Nick was actually enjoying himself, whereas he often found buying trips tedious.

He reached for her hand, forcing her to unfold her arms, and then gave her fingers an affectionate squeeze. He was still holding her hand when they reached their destination.

The hotel where Nick had booked their rooms was nicer than anything Darcie would have chosen had she been picking up the tab herself. It went without saying that it was nicer than anything Stavros would have provided as part of the all-inclusive tour.

Their rooms were on the third floor, which like all of the floors, was open to the atrium on the main level. They made plans to meet for a late dinner, which would give them both a chance to unpack and unwind.

"Wear the white dress to dinner," he suggested as he handed her a key card.

"I didn't buy the white dress."

"What is in there then?" He pointed to two bags she carried that were printed with the shop's logo.

She smiled benignly. "I guess you'll just have to wait and see."

When Darcie said it, she was referring to the sexy wine-colored dress. But that changed when she slipped into her room and realized that it joined with Nick's via an interior door. Because she could quite vividly picture him on the other side of it, undressing, she decided to go for a swim. The hotel had a nice pool in a courtyard outdoors. A quick dip and a little lounging on one of the chaises might be the perfect distraction.

She eyed the tank-style one-piece in a bland shade of blue that she'd brought with her from Athens before deciding to slip into the red bikini. She wouldn't wear it downstairs. Probably. But…

She had just finished tying the top's knot behind her neck when a tapping sounded on the interior door. She grabbed her robe, hastily pulled it on before going to answer it. Her mouth went dry at the sight that greeted her. Nick's shirt was open, the buckle of his belt hung to one side of his unbuttoned trousers. The man was built like a god, with ripped abs and the kind of chest that it seemed a sin to cover with a shirt. This was why she'd decided to go for a swim. This was exactly how she'd pictured him looking.

"I interrupted you," she said.

"I believe I am the one who knocked." He sounded amused, but his expression was intense, aroused.

"R-right. I knew that."

"Is this what you plan to wear to dinner?"

She shook her head and managed to drag some air into

her lungs. She had one hand on the doorjamb and plunked the other one on her hip. "Terry cloth is a little too casual, I think."

"You will not hear me complain."

She laughed softly.

"But I am disappointed."

"Oh?"

"I see red." He reached out and plucked at the bow that peeked from the collar of the robe. "You promised to model *everything* for me."

"I offered. You left."

"Because we were in public," he reminded her. "Will you keep your promise now?"

She swallowed. Nodded. And nearly forgot how to breathe when he loosened the robe's belt.

"Do you like it?" she found the courage to ask.

"Take off the robe."

She did as instructed. The robe slipped from her shoulders and pooled at her feet.

"Well?" She tilted her head to one side and managed a smile.

Nick, however, did not smile. Nor did he say anything. He acted, swiftly and decisively. One minute Darcie was on her side of the door, posing provocatively in the itty-bitty red two-piece. The next she was in his room, pinned between his hard body and the wall while his mouth devoured hers.

"I'm taking this to mean you like what you see," she told him on a breathy laugh when the kiss finally ended.

"I do indeed."

"I was thinking about going swimming. You know, in the hotel pool. Um, that's why I'm wearing my bathing suit."

"Is that why?" he asked. He had maneuvered her away from the wall and was now slowly walking her backward toward the bed.

"Why else?" she asked innocently, even as the edge of the mattress pressed into the back of her thighs.

"I think you put on your bikini to torture me." He stepped back far enough so that he could do a slow inspection of her body. A groan of approval vibrated from his throat.

"I didn't know you were going to knock on my door," she pointed out. "So, that's merely a bonus."

Darcie was amazed at her boldness. Not only did she feel comfortable standing nearly naked before him, but she also felt sexy and confident. She planted her hands on her hips and turned slowly side to side before presenting him with her back and glancing flirtatiously over one shoulder.

"So, you like my suit, hmm?"

His gaze skimmed down a second time and he let out a low whistle. "The suit, what little of it there is, is nice. I like the way you look in it, Darcie. You are beautiful."

Better yet, she felt that way. Smiling in earnest, she asked, "So, are we going?"

"Wh-where?" he stammered.

In addition to looking turned on, Nick looked off balance. Darcie's confidence shot up another notch.

"Swimming." She grinned. "You remembered to pack a pair of trunks, right?"

"I did."

"Good. Put them on."

She slipped around him and started for the door, but only managed two steps before his hands clamped on her waist and she was hauled back against his rock-hard chest, abs and...

In the mirror that hung on the opposite wall, their gazes met. Neither one of them was smiling now. The time for humor and teasing had passed. Nick brushed her hair aside and nuzzled her neck a moment, then his hand came up, his fingers fiddled at the nape of her neck. The knot in the bikini's halter went slack.

"It appears that your top has come loose," he murmured huskily.

He gathered both sides in his hands, holding them at her collarbone. If he were to let go…

"So I see, although I believe it had a little help."

"I can retie it," he offered.

She met his gaze without blinking. She thought she might have stopped breathing, too. "Have you got any other suggestions?"

His hands moved lower, slowly exposing more of her skin inch by inch. They both watched his progress in the mirror.

"I can stop. I *should* stop." His eyes pinched closed a moment and he uttered an oath before pulling the straps taut and retying them. At her questioning gaze in the mirror, he said, "My grandmother thinks I am chivalrous. This is a moment that calls for such old-fashioned thinking."

"It is?"

He turned her to face him, framed her face with his hands. "I want you, Darcie. But I…we…" He pulled his hands away and started stalking around the room. The rest of his explanation was in Greek. Oddly enough, she thought she understood what he meant.

"I only have another week left in Greece."

"Yes. But it is more than that."

A lump formed in her throat. It was?

"Remember when we spoke of your life being at a crossroads?" he asked.

"I said it was more like a busy intersection without a working traffic light."

"In other words, dangerous. Which is why we are going slowly."

There was slow and there was snail-like. "I thought you

saw me as adventurous for wanting to rush across and hope for the best."

"I have changed my mind."

"Worried I could get hurt?" she asked with a tilt of her head.

He didn't answer her question, at least not directly. Instead he said, "The stakes have gotten higher. For both of us. Do you understand?"

Her heart gave an unsteady thump. She knew she had been developing strong feelings for Nick. Real feelings. Feelings that could make walking away from a casual fling in a week very difficult. But until now she hadn't thought Nick might feel the same way. Or that having those feelings might be a problem for him. She knew Nick didn't do more than casual, not since Selene. Darcie sighed. "I think so. Now what?"

He expelled a gusty breath and asked, "Do you still want to go for a swim?"

"Sure. You?"

"Yes." He kissed her cheek before adding, "If I am lucky, the pool will be very, very cold."

Nick got his wish. The water was chilly, especially compared to the hot afternoon air. He and Darcie had the pool to themselves and they stayed in it for nearly an hour. Even so, it wasn't long enough to counteract the effect simply being near her was having on him.

It wasn't only lust he felt when it came to Darcie, which was why he begrudgingly had retied her bikini top and hustled her out of his hotel room. Other emotions were involved that made the prospect of a mere holiday fling less and less appealing.

He liked her. He respected her intelligence, her drive, her resilience. The last thing he wanted was to be responsible for her returning home filled with regrets. That was where chivalry had come in. But self-preservation, he could admit, played a role, too.

So much had happened between the pair of them in such a short time. The feelings Darcie inspired were not unwelcome, but they were unexpected. He'd meant it when he said the stakes had gotten higher for both of them.

Now what?

The question Darcie had asked earlier haunted him. He had no clear answer.

CHAPTER TEN

DARCIE YAWNED AND stretched as she lay on the bed in Nick's guestroom. The sun had crested the horizon a few minutes earlier, but she had been awake for more than an hour listening to the distant sound of fishing boats heading out of the harbor.

Since her and Nick's return from Meteora, time had passed much too quickly for her liking. She blamed it on their busy schedule, which was a combination of business and pleasure. Lots and lots of pleasure, even if it stopped just short of actual sex. In addition to doing research on the internet and writing articles for the auction brochure, she and Nick had met with a deep-pocketed repeat client who was eager to add a 1950s-era, American-made muscle car to his already expansive collection of automobiles, and a new client looking to score his first vintage Porsche.

They also had managed a couple more sightseeing day trips on Greece's mainland, and they'd spent one glorious afternoon lazing on a beach on the island of Andros. She'd worn the bikini again. And she'd known from Nick's expression that he loved seeing her in it, whatever the cost to him personally.

Darcie was having the time of her life. It didn't matter what she and Nick did. She enjoyed being with him and talking to him, whether about the automobiles she was researching or movies they'd seen or current happenings in the world. It amazed her, really, how much they had in common for two people who had grown up in different cultures on different sides of the world.

As for their relationship, she wasn't quite sure how to categorize it. *Fling* didn't fit since the word implied sex. She and Nick hadn't had sex, although she swore that every moment she spent in his company qualified as foreplay. She enjoyed kissing him, the exquisite torture of feeling his mouth and hands on her skin. But she wanted more.

On a frustrated sigh, she rolled to her side and hugged a pillow to her chest. She'd never met another man who made her feel more desirable or quite so aware of her femininity. Yet since Meteora and their brush with physical intimacy in his hotel room, Nick had shown the kind of restraint possessed by the monks who lived in the terra-cotta-tile-roofed monasteries they'd toured the following day. No matter how far things progressed between them physically, he always stopped just short of taking her to bed. Now their time together in Greece was almost over.

Part of Darcie acknowledged that maybe it was just as well they hadn't had sex. Physical intimacy would complicate things, at least on her end. As she'd told Nick, she wasn't the sort of woman to fall in bed with a man simply to scratch an itch.

But another part of her ached to be with him in every sense of the word, no matter how short their time together.

She wasn't on the rebound, as her family might assume. Nor was she confused or vulnerable over her breakup with Tad. Indeed, Darcie had never felt clearer on her reasons for ending her engagement, despite her ex's continuing messages, the most recent of which had been surprisingly conciliatory in tone. Tad wanted her back. He wanted to work things out. But Darcie knew no matter how much he was willing to change, she already had changed more.

There was no going back, even if in a matter of days, she would be flying home to Buffalo. She wouldn't be returning to her old life. The old Darcie was gone. The new Darcie wasn't going to settle and make do. That almost made up for the fact that her idyllic vacation with Nick was coming to an end.

Would they see each other again? That was the million-dollar question, and it weighed heavily on her mind.

Not long after she returned to the United States, he would as well. From what she knew of his schedule, he would leave Greece the day after Pieter's wedding. But even without an ocean to separate them, she and Nick would hardly be neighbors. Besides, he had made no mention of getting together once they were both back in America.

Sure, at one point early in their acquaintance he had offered to show Darcie the sights should she ever find herself in the Big Apple again, but the offer had been more polite than anything else, and he hadn't made a similar one since then, much less issued a formal invitation.

In fact, the more involved they had become the less was said about what the future held for the two of them. Personally, at least. Nick made it plain how pleased he was with the features she'd written for his upcoming auction brochure.

"Use my name as a reference if you think it will help," he'd told her.

He'd also given her the contact information for the editor of an online car collectors' blog that sometimes used freelance writers. Why not? she thought. Clips were clips and the more experience under her belt the better.

Overall, Darcie was pretty satisfied with the work she'd done while in Greece. It wasn't going to win her any Pulitzers, but it was a start, a first step in a new and exciting journey.

She had one last feature to write for Nick for an upcoming auction brochure. The car was a 1914 Packard 4-48. The owner lived in New Jersey and was selling it to finance his daughter's college tuition. Nick had inspected the Packard prior to his trip to Greece and estimated it could bring in up to half a million dollars. He agreed with Darcie that, with the right buyer, the sixty-horsepower touring phaeton might bring in even more since many of its parts were original. That was what made her articles every bit as important as the photographs included in the brochures that would be sent out in advance of the auction.

Darcie tossed the pillow aside and rose. She might as well start to work on it. She was nearly finished with the article and was making a second pot of coffee when the doorbell rang. Nick's appearance was unexpected, even though they had plans for later in the day.

When she opened the door, his gaze swept down to her toes before returning to her face.

"You are dressed."

"And you were hoping otherwise."

He didn't bother to hide his smile. "I was. It's why I didn't call first."

"Sorry to disappoint you then."

"Did I say I was disappointed?" He yanked her into his arms for a hard, fast kiss. While she was still recovering from it, he said, "I have a favor to ask."

"After kissing me like that you can ask me anything."

He made a humming sound and she swore his pupils dilated. "Anything?"

Darcie was playing with fire, but she no longer cared. She wanted to feel not just the heat, but the burn. "Anything."

The devil was in his eyes when he asked, "My grand-mother has invited us for coffee. Do you want to go?"

The mention of his *yiayia* threatened to put a damper on seduction. She thumped his chest with the back of her hand. *"That's* the question you come up with? Seriously?"

His lips quirked. "Not the only one, but I would like to know your answer." Darcie was wearing the turquoise tunic she'd purchased in Trikala. It had a peasant-style neckline that closed with a ribbon tie. Nick fiddled with the ends of the ribbon as he added, "First."

Her brows shot up. First sounded promising.

Still, she asked, "Will the rest of your family be there? I want to know exactly how large of an audience to expect for this command performance."

He shook his head. "My mother is with Selene and her mother—some last-minute wedding preparations. My father and Pieter are working today. It will just be Yiayia."

"All right," she said slowly.

"We will not stay long," he promised. "Afterward, I thought we could ride the cable car to the top of Lycabettus. The view from the hilltop is even better than that from the Acropolis."

It would be the last touristy thing Darcie did in Greece, but that wasn't why she frowned. "Nick, about spending more time with your grandmother, I really like her, which makes me feel—"

He stopped her with another kiss. This one was slower, deeper, sweeter. By the time he finished, they were fully inside his house with the door closed behind him and the foyer wall against Darcie's back.

"If it helps, I am as uncomfortable as you are with the charade, but it is not all an act now." He tipped her chin up. "Is it?"

"It was never *all* an act."

"Exactly. We might not have met when and where we said we did, but I have not lied to them about my feelings. I have always been attracted to you physically, but it is more than that now. Yes?"

"For both of us," she agreed.

"Which brings me to my other question," he said softly.

Darcie could barely breathe, but she managed to say, "And that is?"

Nick tugged on the tunic's ribbon until it gave way. The neckline gaped open, offering a tantalizing glimpse of cleavage.

"May I please make love to you?"

A chorus of *Hallelujah!* rang in her head, but she couldn't keep from asking, "Right now?"

He flicked open the button on her capris. "Right now. I can wait no longer."

They arrived at his grandmother's house two hours later. Darcie was still tingling all over from the best orgasm she'd ever experienced. At one point she hadn't known whether to laugh out loud or start to cry. She'd done neither, thank goodness. Nor had she burst into song, though the lyrics to U2's "Beautiful Day" had been on the tip of her tongue.

As Nick shifted the car into Park, she checked her reflection in her compact mirror for the third time.

"You look the same as you did five minutes ago. In other words, perfect," he assured her, leaning over to give her a kiss.

"I feel…conspicuous," Darcie replied. "Like your grandmother is going to take one look at me and *know* what we were doing less than an hour ago."

"There is no need to worry. She might suspect, but she will not *know*." Nick winked.

"Gee, thanks. That puts my mind at ease."

* * *

"Something about you is different," Yiayia said to Darcie the moment she and Nick walked through the door.

Darcie felt her face flame scarlet and she shot Nick a panicked look.

He put his arm around her shoulders and said mildly, "Greece agrees with her."

Yiayia's expression was shrewd. "Something agrees with her." Then she motioned with her hand. "Come. We will eat outside. The day is too nice to sit in the kitchen."

They followed her through the house and out to the veranda. Darcie took a seat in the shade of the pergola. The midday air was heavy with the scent of roses.

"I made *koulourakia portokaliou* just this morning. I have the recipe for you." She sent Darcie a wink.

"Thank you," Darcie said.

"Are you excited for the wedding?" Yiayia asked as she poured the tea. "Selene and Pieter's wedding, that is."

The older woman's smile turned wily.

"Weddings are exciting," Darcie evaded. She nibbled a cookie.

"What color is the dress you will wear?"

"My dress. Oh, um…" She glanced at Nick for help.

"Darcie wants it to be a surprise."

Yiayia frowned at that, but couldn't resist offering a little unsolicited advice.

"You should wear a bright color. Do not be afraid to stand out. When I was a young woman, I favored red. I was wearing red the night Nicolas's grandfather saw me at a dance. He said the color caught his attention even before I did. For every anniversary my Alexandros gave me red roses." She sighed.

"How long were you married?" Darcie asked.

"Thirty-seven years. It has been twenty-three years since

I lost him. But it feels like yesterday that I was a young woman planning my own wedding." She patted Darcie's hand. "Time passes too quickly. Now my grandchildren are falling in love and getting married."

Falling in love…was that what was happening to Darcie? The assessment felt alarmingly right. Her gaze connected with Nick's. His expression was one she could not read.

"What about you, Yiayia?" he asked then. "What color will you wear to the wedding?"

Now a smile lurked around the corners of his mouth. Darcie knew it was because his grandmother always wore black.

Yiayia pointed a finger at him and smiled. "It is to be a surprise."

They all laughed.

Then Yiayia asked, "Have you ever been to a Greek wedding?"

Finally, a question Darcie could answer with complete honesty. "No. Never."

"Ah, then you are in for a treat. It is too bad you will not see Selene ride the donkey to church, but there will be video to watch later."

"A donkey?" Darcie tried to picture the lovely young woman she'd met perched atop an animal in her wedding day finery. The image simply wouldn't come.

"It is a tradition that represents the bride leaving home," Nick explained. "Her family and friends will walk with her."

"It sounds like fun."

"You wait until you have your turn on the donkey. You will not think so," Yiayia warned. "The donkey I rode, he wanted to run. My father had to hold the rein tight to make him go slow. My mother said it was because the animal knew how eager I was to get to the church."

Once again, they all laughed. The good humor didn't last

long. It vanished as soon as the older woman asked Darcie, "Has Nikolos told you about the *koumbaro*?"

"Yiayia." His voice was uncharacteristically sharp.

But his grandmother was undeterred. She briefly explained it to Darcie, including the custom with the switching of the crowns.

"It sounds lovely," Darcie replied, unsure what else to say. Meanwhile, Nick's expression had grown pinched. If Sophia noticed, she chose to ignore it.

"It also is a special honor that Pieter has asked of Nikolos, but he refuses."

"Yiayia," he said again. This time, his tone was not sharp, but sad, pained.

"After we met you, Darcie, and we saw with our own eyes how you and Nikolos are together, we all hoped..." Yiayia's shoulders rose in a shrug as her voice trailed off.

"I will not do it. I cannot," Nick said. "I would feel... foolish. I feel foolish as it is given all of the talk surrounding Pieter, Selene and me."

"Pride, Nikolos? That is what keeps you from saying yes? Even now that you have found love again yourself, you will not relent? You choose to keep your pride and begrudge Pieter and Selene their happiness?"

"Yiayia—"

But she wasn't through. "Have you no forgiveness in your heart for your only brother?"

"I..." He frowned, unable to finish.

The tension that followed was so thick a machete would have had a hard time hacking through it. It was just as well that Darcie and Nick left soon afterward. The tea and cookies had begun to churn in her stomach.

She said nothing on the drive to where they would catch the cable car to Lycabettus, and during their tour of St. George's Chapel she kept the conversation focused on archi-

tecture and history. At that point, it was really more mono-
logue than conversation. Nick contributed very little. Even
when they stopped at a tavern for a cold drink before heading back down the hillside, he remained unnaturally quiet
and circumspect. It was like the drive to Trikala, only worse.

Obviously, he was troubled by what his grandmother
had said. Was it merely Nick's pride that was injured? Did
he still feel so betrayed by his brother that he was unwill-
ing to act as his *koumbaro*? Or did Nick continue to harbor
tender feelings for Selene?

They were in the cable car, descending from the hilltop,
when he surprised her by bringing her hand to his mouth
and planting a kiss on the back of it.

"What was that for?"

"An apology. I have not been very good company today."

"You have a lot on your mind."

"Yes." He nodded, then added, "Thank you, Darcie."

She blinked at that. "For what?"

"For not pushing me on this matter the way my family is."

She managed a smile. Those questions she had would go
unasked and unanswered.

For the second morning in a row, a knock sounded at the
door as Darcie was making a pot of coffee. Nick. Her heart
picked up speed and her body temperature shot up by several degrees as she recalled the tenderness with which he'd
made love to her the night before. Where that first coupling
during the day had been frenzied and rushed, Nick had been
exquisitely slow and thorough the second time.

As for those questions that had troubled Darcie earlier
in the day, they were forgotten. Surely, the man who made
such sweet love to her could not still love someone else.

She was smiling as she opened the door, a comment

about being insatiable ready on her lips. But it wasn't Nick who stood on the stoop. It was Selene.

"Forgive me for being so rude and not calling first," the other woman said in halting English. She smiled nervously as she clutched her handbag to her chest. "I hope I did not catch you at a bad time."

"No. Not at all," Darcie replied, trying not to feel self-conscious in a pair of jersey cotton shorts and a tank top that doubled as her sleepwear.

Thank goodness she had at least dragged a brush through her hair and rubbed the sleep from her eyes. Meanwhile, Selene looked picture-perfect in a cotton skirt and sleeveless blouse. Even in a pair of high heels, she barely came to Darcie's shoulder. The old Darcie would have slouched. This Darcie squared her shoulders and settled her hands on her "good birthing hips."

"May I come in?" Selene asked.

"Of course." Darcie stepped aside. It seemed odd to be welcoming Nick's former girlfriend and soon-to-be sister-in-law into his house, but neither woman commented on it. "I just poured myself coffee. Would you like some?"

"Please."

They made their way to the kitchen, where Darcie got a cup down from one of the cupboards.

"I don't know how to use a *briki*. I hope this is okay," she said, pouring from the carafe of the automatic coffeemaker.

"This is fine. Thank you." After stirring in an obscene amount of sugar, Selene took a delicate sip. To her credit, her grimace was barely detectable.

Darcie sipped her own coffee. Silence ensued as the women eyed one another.

"So…" Darcie expelled a breath.

"This is very…"

"Awkward."

"Yes. You must be wondering why I am here."

"Um, a little," Darcie admitted. She didn't ask if Selene had ever been in Nick's home before. Quite honestly, she didn't want to know.

"As you must be aware, there is a…strain between Pieter and Nick. It goes back years to when…when Pieter and I began to date."

"Because you used to date Nick," Darcie added, figuring it best not to tiptoe around the big white elephant sitting in the center of the room.

Selene closed her eyes briefly, nodded. She looked miserable. Ridiculously put-together and gorgeous, but miserable all the same.

"Pieter is…I do not know the English word to describe it." Selene set her coffee down on the counter and paced to the window. "He loves his brother very much."

"I'm not trying to be rude, but *you* loved Nick at one time, too."

"I did or at least I thought so. Nick and I, we were so young when we began seeing each other. I was a teenager, barely one year out of school. I thought I knew my heart, but my feelings for him changed as time passed."

Darcie was in no position to cast stones. After all, she'd thought she'd loved Tad. She'd accepted his proposal of marriage and then had spent six years making wedding plans, a couple of those years living under the same roof. She'd been a lot older than Selene at the time, too.

"You didn't want to relocate to another country."

Selene shook her head. "I love it here. Greece is…home."

"It must have been difficult when you realized how you felt about Pieter."

Selene nibbled her lower lip. "It happened…slowly. At least for me. Pieter and I have known each other for so long. We started as friends. After Nick moved to New York and we broke up, Pieter would call. Checking up on me, he said." Her expression turned soft and her smile was nostalgic. "We started meeting at a café in town after work for coffee. Then it became drinks at a tavern in the evening. At first, we talked about Nick. How much we both missed him. Then we just talked. About everything."

"And you realized how much you had in common," Darcie said, her thoughts turning to Nick.

"Yes. We liked the same things. We *wanted* the same things in life."

"You were falling in love." Darcie wanted to ignore the voice whispering that she was in the same predicament. Could this really be the Big L?

"The first time Pieter kissed me, I had never felt that way before. Then he told me he loved me and confessed that he had been in love with me for a very long time. We both cried, because by now I was in love, too. But..." Selene pinched her eyes shut. When she opened them, they were bright with unshed tears. "I never meant to come between brothers."

Darcie didn't doubt the other woman's sincerity. Selene's pain was nearly palpable. Still, she felt the need to point out, "All the same, Nick felt betrayed. He trusted Pieter."

"Pieter never betrayed Nick's trust. Nick and I were no longer a couple. Even though we had done nothing wrong, we both felt guilty at first. We even stopped seeing each other for several weeks, but..." She lifted her shoulders. "Eventually, we could not deny what was in our hearts."

"I'm happy for you." How could Darcie be otherwise? "But I'm not sure I understand what this has to do with me."

"Pieter's mother and grandmother have tried to bridge the gap between the brothers."

"By trying to set Nick up on dates," Darcie mused. "He told me."

"They did not know about you at the time," Selene hastened to add.

"I know." How could they?

"They want him to be happy. That is what we all have wanted for him. And now he is. He has found love again."

Selene smiled. Darcie nearly choked. She rested a hand on her chest. Her heart beat unsteadily beneath it.

"About that, I don't know that I can claim the credit." Could she?

"I do not understand what you mean."

"Nick and I haven't been seeing each other for very long." As in less than two weeks. And even though they'd made love, neither of them had attached a label to their feelings.

"The length of time does not matter. He *is* happy. Anyone who knows him can see that."

Okay, Darcie would give her that. And she had to admit, she was pretty darned happy, herself. But... "It's not like you and Pieter."

And it wasn't. Not by a long shot since they would be saying goodbye soon, and their future, assuming they even had one, was far from determined.

Selene was nodding. "I understand. Pieter and I denied we were in love at first, too."

"Oh, hey. Look, I'm not denying anything. It's just that... and Nick and I aren't...he hasn't said..." She swallowed.

Selene's smile was serene. "He loves you, even if he has not said so. Yiayia is right about the two of you."

Darcie squinted at Selene through one eye. She was going to regret it, but she had to know. "What is Yiayia saying?"

"She has seen the way Nick looks at you. The way you look at each other. She says it is a good sign."

Even as Darcie's heart kicked out a few extra beats, she was protesting, "But I'm not Greek!"

"And *still* Yiayia likes you!" Selene chuckled softly before sobering. "Our wedding is in just two days. The only gift Pieter and I want, the only one that truly matters, is Nick's blessing."

Uh-oh. "I don't know what you expect me to do, Selene."

The young woman reached across the table and took Darcie's hand in both of hers. "If you could just talk to him. Please."

"It's not my place." And hadn't Nick already thanked her for staying out of it and not pushing? But Selene looked so heartbroken, Darcie found herself softening. "What would I say to him? What could I possibly say that Pieter and the rest of the family haven't already?"

"I do not know," Selene admitted on a ragged sigh. She let go of Darcie's hand and rose. "I am sorry to have bothered you."

"It was no bother. Really."

They were at the door when Selene said, "At least Nick will be at the wedding. For a while that seemed doubtful. Even with you at his side, I know this will not be pleasant for him."

Darcie swallowed. She wouldn't be there. He would be on his own.

Selene was saying, "Perhaps I am being selfish in wanting more for Pieter's sake."

Her words struck a chord in Darcie. *For Pieter's sake.* Not her own.

"Love isn't selfish," Darcie murmured when the door had closed.

Nick had told her that very thing after his argument with Pieter. At the time, he'd seemed to be examining his old reasons behind the brothers' feud. She had an idea.

Darcie hadn't pushed, but she cared about Nick too much not to offer a little nudge.

CHAPTER ELEVEN

Something was on Darcie's mind, but Nick couldn't figure out what. Women were rarely a mystery to him. But then, Darcie had been from the very beginning. Not mysterious in the way some of the women he'd dated back in New York tried to be. Darcie wasn't one to play games. For her, seduction wasn't an art that she practiced. She came by it naturally.

Nick would be lying if he said he hadn't enjoyed the little pieces of herself she'd revealed in their short time together. Or if he said he wasn't looking forward to seeing, learning more. All of which made her looming departure from Greece more disconcerting. Their time together had been amazing and sweet, and was proving all too brief. Already he was trying to think of ways to prolong it. But to what end? The answer he kept coming up with left him staggered.

Was he falling in love?

For her last night in Athens, Nick had made reservations for dinner at one his favorite restaurants, determined to show her a wonderful time and, as a side bonus, to keep his own mind off the fact that his brother's rehearsal dinner was that same evening. Nick had no official role in the wedding, but he'd still been invited. Both he and Darcie had.

"That sounds nice," Darcie said when he had called to confirm their plans. Then she'd thrown him completely when she added, "But you need to cancel the reservation. I've decided I'm going to make dinner for you here."

"You are? And what will be for dessert?" he'd asked.

"I think you know."

She'd sounded a little breathless. And Nick had been torturing himself ever since with fantasies of her prancing about his kitchen, wearing a little white apron and nothing else.

When he arrived at the house just after five o'clock, however, the kitchen was missing both a cook and a meal. Darcie was on the terrace, reclining on one of the chaise lounges with a glass of chilled wine in her hand. Her eyes were closed, her face tilted toward the sun. She was wearing a tank top and shorts that ended high on her thighs and her tanned legs looked ridiculously long. Her feet were bare. Her toenails painted a festive shade of tangerine.

"I thought you were making dinner?"

"That was just part of my ploy to lure you here."

He leaned over and captured her smiling lips for a long, thorough kiss. "Should I be worried for my safety?" he asked as he straightened.

In answer, she set aside her wine, grabbed his tie and tugged him back for a second kiss.

His breathing ragged, he said, "Perhaps we should take this inside and skip ahead to that dessert you promised."

"Sorry." She sounded seriously contrite. "I'm afraid there's no time. You'll be late."

"For?"

"Dinner."

He couldn't think straight with his hormones staging a riot. A common occurrence around Darcie. "I canceled our reservations, remember?"

She inhaled deeply before letting out her breath. "I'm not

talking about the restaurant. I'm talking about Pieter and Selene's rehearsal dinner."

He snagged the wine she'd set down and took a sip, stalking to the terrace's rail. "I am not going."

Darcie stood and joined him at the railing. "I want you to reconsider. In fact, I am asking you to."

"Why?"

"Because if you don't go, Nick, you're going to regret it. Just as you will regret not playing a meaningful role in their wedding."

"It is not as simple as that!" he shouted.

But Darcie was undeterred. "I'm not saying everything will magically be all better. But it's a start. This rift between you and your brother, it will never truly begin to mend otherwise."

"And to think I thanked you for not interfering," he said dryly as his temper began to simmer. He shoved a hand through his hair. "I know you mean well, but this is not your business, Darcie. You are a tourist here on holiday. This is my life!"

She didn't back down, even if just for a moment she looked as if she'd been slapped. "I may only be a tourist, Nick, but your family thinks otherwise, which is why Selene came to see me."

Nick didn't bother to mask his surprise. "Selene was here? What did she want from you?"

"From me? Nothing." Darcie waited a beat. "What she wants is something only you can give. She wants you and Pieter to be brothers again. In short, what she wants, Nick, is your blessing on their marriage. Not for her sake, mind you. For Pieter's. Love isn't selfish, remember?"

Nick swallowed. He recognized the lump lodged in his throat as guilt, and that was before Darcie said, "Selene asked if I would talk to you. She thought you might listen to me since we're supposedly a couple. You know what?" Darcie poked a finger in his chest. "I got the feeling that she would have gotten down on her knees and begged if she felt it necessary. It is that important to her. To both of them."

Nick closed his eyes as emotions tumbled fast and furiously inside him. His anger of a moment ago had drained away. As for the betrayal he'd felt for so long, that was gone, too. It had been ebbing for a while now, he knew, the last remnants disappearing as he'd gotten to know Darcie. The emotion that remained was undiluted shame. He hung his head as it crashed over him like a rogue wave.

"I'm sorry." Darcie's hand was on his back, her touch tentative. Where a moment ago her tone had been confrontational, it was apologetic now as she said, "I don't mean to cause you more pain, and I know I have no business whatsoever interfering in your personal life, but I said what I said because I care about you. Deeply. I want you to be happy. And, frankly, Nick, in addition to having regrets, you'll never truly move on with your own life until you let go of the past." Her voice hitched when she added, "And you haven't done that."

He turned. "You think I still love Selene?"

"No. Well, maybe I've sort of wondered," she admitted softly. She made her tone light when she added, "I know you're insanely attracted to me and all, but—"

Was that all it was? He didn't think so, but what he really needed Darcie to know right now was the absolute truth. "I do not love Selene."

"Oh. Good. That's *really* good." A smile fluttered briefly on her lips before she added, "But you've held so tightly to the past, Nick, that you're robbing yourself of a future with your brother and the family you clearly adore."

She understood him so well, better than any woman ever had. His conscience flared as he thought of how only a moment earlier he'd called her a tourist just passing through. He owed her an apology, but he didn't trust his voice enough to speak. Darcie apparently took his silence to mean something else and continued.

"You've helped me start over these past couple of weeks. I only wanted to return the favor. For what it's worth, I believe Selene when she says that she and Pieter did everything they could to deny their feelings for one another."

"I know."

"Did you also know that when they realized they were in love they even stopped seeing each other for a while?"

"No." The news didn't sit well with Nick's conscience now that he no longer saw himself in the role of the injured party. He said softly, "I think I always knew Pieter had not set out to betray me."

Just as he knew he had been selfish in his expectations of Selene. Nick had disregarded her feelings to follow his dream. Then, even after they had parted ways, he'd somehow still expected her to change her mind, to—what? Pine for him? Because it would have soothed his pride. He didn't care for what that said about his character.

He turned, caught Darcie's hand in his. His smile reflected the remorse he was feeling.

"My grandmother was right. I have let my pride get in the way of what truly matters. And you are right as well, Darcie. I already have regrets where my brother is concerned. I do not want to have more."

She squinted at him. "So, you're not angry with me for butting in?"

"No. I am angry with myself for many things, including what I said to you just now. A tourist just passing through." He winced as he repeated it. "It was insulting to you and an outright lie. You are so much more than that to me, Darcie. Can you forgive me?"

She kissed him in answer. Afterward, she asked, "Does this mean you are going to the rehearsal dinner?"

"No. It means *we* are going." When she opened her mouth to protest, he said, "Do not even think about backing out. I want you with me. I...*need* you there."

She smiled. "I'm so happy you will give them your blessing. It is the only gift she said they want."

Nick had already swallowed his pride, now he searched his heart and reached a decision.

"I will give them my blessing, but I can think of an even more meaningful gift to offer."

The rehearsal dinner wasn't at a restaurant. Rather, it was at the Costas home. More specifically, in his parents' yard, which had been decorated with white streamers and flowers to fit the occasion.

Even though the actual wedding party was quite small, Nick's mother and grandmother had been cooking for the past two days in preparation of the feast. In addition to his parents and grandmother, the bride-and-groom-to-be, and Selene's parents, of course, only a few friends and close relatives would be in attendance. The size of the audience would make it easier to humble himself, Nick decided.

The house smelled of lamb and simmering vegetables when he and Darcie arrived. She'd been quiet on the drive over, but she'd rested her hand over his on the gearshift and had never let go. Nick appreciated her support. He appreciated *her*. If not for her interference... No, it went further than that. If not for her appearance in his life, what he was about to do would not be occurring. Nick would have jetted back to New York and remained locked in his bitter disillusionment, isolated from his family, angry with the brother who had always been his best friend.

Love is not selfish.

Now, as they walked through the door that opened into the yard, he held her hand tightly, not only because he needed her support, but because he also didn't want to let her go. Ever.

God help him. Nick fully understood his brother's predicament now. Love happened. Even when one didn't go looking for it. Even when the timing was all wrong. It was terrifying and wonderful all at the same time. And denying it served no purpose.

His mother and grandmother were in the kitchen, arguing over the doneness of the roast.

"Nick!" Thea cried out when he and Darcie entered the room.

"Mama." He kissed her cheek, wiped the tears that had started to leak from the corners of her eyes.

"Please tell me you and Darcie will be staying," she whispered hoarsely, hopefully.

"If it is not too much trouble."

She huffed out a breath that served as her answer. "I will set the extra plates on the table."

While Thea bustled to the cupboard and got to work, Yiayia stood rooted in place, her hands clasped in front of her as if praying. She nodded, opened her mouth but said nothing. It was the first time Nick could recall his grandmother being speechless. He kissed her cheek as well.

"I know," he said softly. "I know."

"Do you want me to send Pieter inside so you can speak to him in private?" his mother asked.

It was tempting, but too easy. "No. I will go to him." Taking a deep breath, he extended a hand to Darcie. "Will you come with me?"

"You don't need to ask."

Conversations dried up midsentence when he and Darcie stepped out into the yard. Selene's parents, who he had not seen in years, looked horrified at first, as if they feared Nick was there to make a scene.

"Nick!" Selene called. Then her hand shot to her mouth, as if she wasn't sure she should draw attention to his arrival.

Nick's gaze cut to his brother, who was standing beside her. Pieter's eyes grew wide in surprise. Afterward, he neither smiled nor frowned. His expression remained wary, although Nick told himself he saw hope flicker in his brother's eyes as he closed the distance that separated them.

"Hello, Pieter. I hope I am not too late."

"Dinner has not yet started."

"That is not what I mean," Nick said quietly. "I hope I am not too late to repair the damage my stubbornness has done."

The stiffness left Pieter's shoulders. His mouth curved in a smile. "You know better than to ask."

In an instant, he had made his way around the table and was embracing Nick.

"Thank you," Pieter whispered.

"One more thing," Nick said afterward. "If you still want me to act as your *koumbaro*, I would be honored."

"There is only one thing to say to that," Pieter replied before shouting, *"Opa!"*

"I am sorry, Pieter." Nick transferred his gaze to Selene then. Long ago, he'd thought he would spend the rest of his life with her. Even after their breakup, after he'd understood how ill-suited they were, he'd refused to accept how perfectly suited she was to Pieter. When he started to apologize, however, she stopped him with a shake of her head.

"The past is the past, Nick."

For once, they were all in agreement.

"Pieter and Selene are so happy," Darcie commented as Nick drove her back to his house later that evening.

She got misty-eyed just thinking about how the brothers had embraced and the joy on Thea and George's faces after Nick agreed to act as Pieter's *koumbaro* at the service. She wished she would be there to see it.

As if he could read her mind, Nick said, "I know you are scheduled to fly back to the States, but I would like for you to attend the wedding with me."

It's what his family was expecting. What they had been expecting since the first time they met Darcie. Only she and Nick had known that her flight was scheduled to depart before the nuptials ever occurred and that he had intended to attend on his own.

"My family will be disappointed if you are not there to share in the celebration. They credit you for making me come to my senses, you know." He cast a smile in her direction, and then sobered. "I do, as well."

Something about his expression was different. Darcie couldn't quite put a finger on it. "I think you would have eventually."

"Perhaps. But not in time for their wedding. Not in time to ease their hearts with my blessing or to act as my brother's best man. So, will you come with me, Darcie?"

"I want to, Nick," she said slowly.

He studied her a moment. "Saying that you want to is not the same as saying you will. Please say yes."

Darcie took a deep breath and gave herself over to fate. "Yes."

"You're staying in Greece?"

"Sheesh, Becks, you make it sound like I'm moving here for good," Darcie replied on a laugh. "It's only for an extra couple of days. You and I will still meet for coffee and gossip when I get back. It will just have to wait until Tuesday now."

Darcie had already called her father with similar news since he had volunteered to pick her up at the airport. He'd taken the change to her itinerary in stride, probably because Darcie had left him with the impression it was the result of the airline overbooking her return flight. She felt a little guilty about that, but figured the white lie was better than having him worry.

Becky, however, wasn't buying it.

"What's really going on? And, no, I will not wait until Tuesday for an explanation. I want to know right now."

"Okay." Darcie sighed. "You know how I mentioned before that Nick and his brother were estranged, and the rift between them was a source of friction for the entire family?"

"Uh-huh. You said that was why his mother and grandmother kept trying to set him up on dates," Becky said.

"Right. So, he was pretending to be dating me so they would cease and desist."

"Uh-huh. His family wanted Nick to find happiness himself so he would— Oh, my God!"

An ocean away, Darcie could see her friend jumping to conclusions. "Becky, no. It's not—"

But her friend was shouting excitedly, "He's in love with you! That gorgeous Greek man is in love with you!"

"No." Despite the denial, Darcie's heart took off at a gallop. She swallowed and forced it to slow down. "He hasn't said anything about love. He's patched things up with his brother, and now he's asked me to stay and attend the wedding. It's his way of saying thanks, I think. Because...I don't know...I helped him put aside his lingering feelings of betrayal and move on."

"And how do you suppose you managed to do that?" Becky asked, her voice laced with triumph. "The man has moved on...to you! Are you in love with him?"

"I just broke off my engagement." Darcie's protest sounded weak even to her own ears.

"The timing sucks, I'll give you that. But your breakup with Tad was a long time coming, and we both know it."

"Nick and I hardly know one another," Darcie said, well aware that the explanation carried little weight. True in terms of time, they had only just met. In other ways...it was as if she had known him forever. He understood her so well.

"My mom and dad met on a blind date, eloped a month later and have been going strong for thirty-five years."

"Becks—"

"You knew Tad for years, Darcie. *Years!* And you still weren't sure in the end. Doesn't that tell you something? When it's right, it's right. And you just know it. The amount of time doesn't matter."

"I've got to go."

"Darcie—"

"See you Tuesday," she said and quickly disconnected.

She didn't want to talk about it. She didn't want to *think* about it. What Becky suggested was preposterous, outrageous and very, very probable, at least on Darcie's end. As for Nick...well that was a whole other matter.

Rain was forecast for Pieter and Selene's big day. The sky was thick with fat dark clouds when Darcie and Nick entered the church, but nothing could dampen the excitement of the guests assembled in the church's pews. When the bride started up the aisle, all eyes were on her, and even the insistent tapping of rain against the stained-glass windows was ignored. Selene made a gorgeous bride. And she was so obviously in love.

Darcie had never attended a Greek wedding, but in many ways it was not so different from the American ones she had attended, even if she didn't understand much of what was being said. Love and commitment, such things were universal. At Nick's family's insistence, she was seated in the front row, wedged between his mother and grandmother. Even before the ceremony started, Sophia had stuffed a lace-edged hankie into her hand.

"You will need this," the older woman predicted.

Thea had nodded, dabbing her eyes.

Nick, of course, was on the altar with the bride and groom during the exchange of vows. He looked as handsome as ever in formal attire, his dark hair tamed for the event. As the *koumbaro*, he placed the crowns on their heads at the appointed time, and then switched them back and forth three times to symbolize their union.

Darcie might not have understood the words being spoken but the emotions translated perfectly. She found herself sniffling and dabbing at her eyes right along with Thea and Sophia, grateful for the hankie.

"Thank you," Nick's mother whispered to Darcie as the bride and groom shared their first kiss as husband and wife. "You have given me back my sons."

"I...oh. Actually, Nick—"

"Nick is so happy." Thea smiled. "Maybe soon Pieter will be switching the crowns on your heads."

Darcie's eyes filled and the tears spilled over. As Thea squeezed her hand, Yiayia wiped them away with a knowing smile.

By the end of the ceremony, the storm had passed. As they left the church for the reception hall, patches of blue were visible in the sky. It was fitting given all that had happened.

Darcie had never enjoyed herself at a wedding reception more, especially when the dancing began. Nick and his family showed her some of the basic steps to traditional Greek dances.

"I'm afraid I have two left feet," she told him after one dance, during which she had stepped on his toes at least half a dozen times.

Now they were seated at a table, enjoying a glass of wine. Darcie had sworn off the ouzo after the first toast. The inside of her throat still felt as if it were on fire from the strong spirit.

"You were doing well for just learning. It takes time."

Time that she didn't have. "I can't believe I'll be going home soon."

"Let's not speak of that now." The band began to play a new song. The melody was familiar, if old. Darcie placed it by the time Nat King Cole started to sing "Unforgettable." Nick stood, held out his hand. "I requested this one especially for you."

"Am I unforgettable?" Darcie found the courage to ask.

"What do you think?"

Gazing into his dark eyes, she chickened out. "I think I have had the best vacation ever, and I'm going to be really sorry to see it end."

On the dance floor, Nick gathered her closer and rested his cheek against hers. It was just as well that he could no longer see her face, because despite Darcie's best efforts, her eyes began to tear.

CHAPTER TWELVE

"IS THIS GOODBYE or is it 'see you later'?" Darcie asked Nick as they sipped coffee in a crowded Newark airport café.

The question had been weighing heavily on both their minds, but Darcie apparently was the only one brave enough to give it voice. Another time her newfound courage might have made her smile. After all, mere weeks ago, she had been a go-along-to-get-along girl. Right now, her transformation took a backseat to heartache.

Her connecting flight to Buffalo wouldn't board for another hour yet. She'd insisted he didn't need to wait with her, but Nick was just as insistent that he would—prolonging the inevitable.

Neither of them had slept on the long flight from Athens. They'd spent the time talking, each sharing details of their lives from the mundane to the profound. Even so, they had scrupulously avoided making any reference to their relationship and the future.

Until now.

"Is there a difference?" he asked.

"You know there is." She gathered up the empty sugar packets and crushed them into a ball. Her gaze was fixed on her fist when she continued. "I'm only asking because if this is the last time I'm likely to see you, I'm going to want to make my kiss count."

"They have *all* counted," he assured her.

"True. Some more than others," she added thinking about their lovemaking.

Back at his home after the wedding, Nick had undressed Darcie slowly, hands caressing her skin as if memorizing her body's every dip and curve. The exquisite tenderness of his touch, the soft cadence of his voice as he spoke in his native tongue, both had been in stark contrast to his fierce expression and ultimate possession.

Afterward, he'd gathered her close.

"Tonight, I will stay," he'd told her. "I want to watch you wake."

True to his word, when Darcie opened her eyes early the next day, Nick had still been beside her and already awake. Indeed, given the shadows under his eyes, she'd wondered if he'd slept at all.

"Just as I suspected," he'd said quietly.

"What?"

"You are even more beautiful in the morning."

So, now, she had to know. "Will we see each other again, Nick? Whatever the answer is, I promise I can handle it. I'm not fragile."

No, Darcie wasn't fragile, but that didn't mean she couldn't be hurt or manipulated. She had been in the past. Nick was determined to do neither. Unfortunately, he found himself in a predicament. The past two weeks had been amazing, so much so that he didn't want them to end. They made for a great beginning. But...

It would be much easier if they lived in the same city. Then they could fully explore their feelings and decide over time where they were heading. But Darcie lived on the other side of the state, which was better than being on the other side of the ocean, but still not close enough for a relationship to develop naturally. As it was, what had occurred between them in Greece had been shaped by outside forces, not the least of which were her broken engagement and his strained family ties.

Now that they were returning to their everyday lives, what would happen? In the light of a new day, would she look back on her time in Greece and see it as a romantic holiday dalliance and nothing more? That was how it had started. That was all it was supposed to be.

Nick didn't wonder how he would feel once he was back in his old routine. He knew. He loved Darcie.

So, he said, "I want to see you again."

"You don't sound happy about that."

"I am being cautious, I suppose. For both of our sakes."

"Are you worried that I'll suddenly realize I still love Tad or that I want to go back to my old job as a fact-checker?" she asked.

"No, but you have choices to make, Darcie. And I don't want to put any added pressure on you."

"I think I've already made those choices."

Nick nodded, somewhat mollified, but he still felt the need to point out, "Darcie, your life is in a state of upheaval. It has been since we met. In a way, you are starting over. I was selfish once. I expected someone else to bend her life to suit my needs. I don't want to do that again. You have so much to sort out right now."

"I need a new address and to revamp my resumé. The rest…" She shrugged. "It will sort out itself."

"Your plane leaves in less than an hour for Buffalo. That is where you live. I am in Manhattan."

"And if I lived in Manhattan, too?"

His heart took off like a shot at the idea. That was Darcie's dream, he knew. To move to New York City and work as a serious journalist. Even as he wanted to offer to help her pack her bags and move that very day, he also knew she needed money to do so, and she wouldn't accept his financial assistance. He'd had a hard enough time convincing her to accept it in Greece, and even then she had insisted on a *quid pro quo* arrangement. But without a reliable source of income, she wouldn't be able to swing New York's high cost of living.

"I want you in New York. Make no mistake about that." He swallowed hard then as he pushed what he wanted behind what would be best for Darcie. "But the city is very expensive, and I am trying to be realistic. Also, your entire family is in Buffalo. When everything is said and done, you may…you may decide that is where you want to stay. I would understand."

It would kill him, but he would understand.

Darcie's smile was reassuring. "I'm not Selene, Nick. I'm not going to change my mind. I *will* come to New York." The smile disappeared then. "But it's going to take a little while, before I have established myself as a writer and can afford to move."

"A little while," he repeated.

They both fell silent.

"And in the meantime?" she asked.

"It is a short flight. I can be in Buffalo every weekend."

"That's a lot of frequent flyer miles," Darcie murmured.

"It won't be forever. Eventually, we will be together in the same city." Even as Nick said it old memories swirled like vultures. He did his best to ignore them, but some of his concern must have shown on his face.

"You're wondering if while we are apart I will reach the conclusion that what happened in Greece was simply meant to stay there," she said softly.

He didn't care for Darcie's assessment, but he couldn't argue its accuracy. "I would understand."

"Because I'm supposedly vulnerable and confused and

we only just met?" She arched an eyebrow. "Oh, please. I spent years with Tad and I never felt for him what I'm starting to feel for you, Nick."

He knew what he was starting to feel, too, but, as much as Nick wanted to give voice to the words, he was afraid. "Absence does not always make the heart grow fonder. Sometimes…feelings change."

Her eyes were bright, but she nodded. "And you think mine will."

"No!" God help him, he hoped not.

"All right. Let's put it to the test."

"What do you mean?"

"We won't see each other until I can afford to move to New York," she said baldly.

Her suggestion caught him off guard. "How long will that be?"

"I don't know," Darcie admitted on a frown.

"Six months," he declared. "That is all the time I will give you." It might take longer than that for her to build her resumé, but half a year was all the time Nick was willing to be apart.

She nodded. Exhaled. "And during that time, we won't see one another."

"No." He swallowed before adding, "Nor will we speak to one another on the telephone."

She nibbled her lower lip. "I assume texting and emails will be out of the question then, too, huh?"

He chuckled in spite of himself. Mirth didn't last long before he sobered. "We will have no contact at all. If I am in contact with you, I will want to *be* with you. My resolve will weaken."

"And that would be bad?"

"Not bad, but…selfish." It kept coming back to that.

"You need time, Darcie. You may not think so, but I want you to have it."

And he wanted her to be sure of her feelings for both of their sakes.

She exhaled slowly and nodded. "Okay. No contact at all. And then what?"

"If after six months we both still feel the same way we will meet."

"Where?" She chuckled as she added, "On the observation deck of the Empire State Building?"

"If that is where you wish."

"That was a joke, Nick. Sorry. Obviously you've never seen *An Affair to Remember* or *Sleepless in Seattle.*"

She quickly explained how the couples in both movies had made plans to meet at the New York landmark.

"I like the idea of a neutral site so there is no pressure, but too many other variables appear left to chance," he said. "I do not want to leave anything to chance where you are concerned."

She smiled. "Then where?"

An idea came to him. "Are you familiar with Tidwell's?"

"The big auction house in Brooklyn that is your main competitor?"

He nodded. "The first Saturday of each month, it auctions classic automobiles. We can meet there in January."

"The start of a new year." She smiled. "I like it. Very symbolic."

If all went as he hoped, it would be the start of much more than a new year. He jotted down the pertinent information on a paper cocktail napkin and handed it to her.

"Remember, we will not be in touch between now and then, so do not lose this."

The smile she gave him now was wobbly. "I've already got it committed to memory."

"If…if you do not come—"

"I'll be there. I'll wear red in honor of your grandmother. If you change your—"

Nick stopped her from finishing the thought with a kiss. Then, with time ticking down until her flight boarded, he walked with her as far as the airport allowed.

"This is not goodbye, so there is no need to make it count," he reminded her as he drew her into his arms.

"That's right. It's see you later. Or, more accurately, see you in six months."

Still, the kiss counted. When it came to Darcie, everything did.

CHAPTER THIRTEEN

DARCIE HAD BEEN back in Buffalo a full week when she saw Tad. She had called him upon her return to the States and left a brief message to let him know she was home safe and sound, and appreciated the concern he'd expressed in his many voice mails. She'd tried to make it clear in her tone that she didn't want to rehash the past, but he showed up at her parents' house one evening anyway.

Becky had been nice enough to let her move in after the breakup, but Darcie couldn't keep imposing on her friend, nor could she afford to pay half the rent if she wanted to save up for New York, which meant she'd moved back in with her parents.

"Tad, it's so good to see you. Isn't it good to see him, Darcie?" Her mother beamed a smile in her direction as they stood in the foyer.

"Come on, hon. Let's leave them alone," her father said. He sent Darcie a wink of encouragement as he led her mother to the kitchen.

"I probably should have called first," Tad said. He smiled weakly. "I guess I didn't want to take the chance that you would tell me not to come. I think we need to talk."

"I think we've said all there is to say."

His expression made it clear he didn't agree.

"I ran in to Becky while you were in Greece. She told me

you'd met someone. A smooth-talking local who was squiring you about Athens because of a little misunderstanding with the tour company."

A little misunderstanding?

"Tad, the company you booked our honeymoon trip with was all but bankrupt. If not for Nick I would have been stranded at the airport and then booking a return flight to Buffalo within two days."

"I'm sorry about that. I'm sorry about a lot of things, Darcie." He reached for her hand. Because it would have been rude to tug it away, she let him hold it while he went on. "When you didn't answer any of the messages I became worried that something had happened to you."

How sweet, she was thinking, until he added, "Or that you'd done something stupid."

"Stupid?"

"You haven't been acting like yourself, Darcie. Your mother mentioned that you're thinking of quitting your job. You love that job."

"I've *tolerated* that job," she corrected. How could he still not understand that? "I've always wanted to be a serious journalist and live in the city."

"I thought you outgrew that dream."

"No."

Tad went on as if she hadn't spoken. "When your mother told me that you'd postponed your return from Greece, I almost booked a flight to Athens."

That came as a surprise. Tad had never been the sort to do anything spontaneous. "Why would you do that?"

"To save you from doing something rash. Given your fragile state of mind and what Becky had said about your tour guide…"

She did tug her hand away now and then crossed her arms over her chest. "My fragile state of mind?"

"You weren't thinking clearly. I hoped by giving you time, you would come to your senses and then we could sit down and have a rational discussion about our future."

She shook her head. Her smile was sad, even if she knew she had made the right decision. "We had plenty of time to talk, Tad. We were engaged for six years. I thought I wanted to be your wife, but—"

"I know you were upset about moving in with my mother. You've made your point. I'm willing to compromise. We can buy our own house. We won't build the addition onto Mother's. She understands." Of course he would have run it by Evelyn first to gain her approval. "Besides, she's only sixty-six and in good health yet. We can revisit our living arrangements in a few years."

"No!" Darcie screamed before moderating her tone. "Look, Tad, I don't want to hurt you, but we aren't getting back together."

The Taylor Swift song played in her head and she nearly added a few *evers* just for emphasis.

"It's the man you met in Greece. He turned you against me," Tad muttered sourly.

Of this much Darcie was certain. "Nick doesn't have anything to do with our breakup. I made that decision before he and I met."

"You're stressed out, confused," Tad insisted. "You don't know what you want. You don't know what you're saying."

"But I do know, Tad. I can't marry you. I'm sorry. I don't love you."

She loved Nick.

Nick's apartment was quieter than he recalled it being, and some of the delight he found in Manhattan definitely was missing. He went about the business of living and working, but the days ticked by slowly and it was a constant struggle not to pick up the phone and call Darcie. He wanted to talk to her or even just hear her voice saying his name.

The brochure she'd helped him with went to the printer. He popped a few copies of it in the mail to her when he got them. That was business and as a contract employee she was entitled to them. As much as he wanted to, he didn't include a personal note, only his business card paper-clipped to the first page of one of the copies. In addition to no phone calls, they were to have no correspondence of any kind. He cursed himself a fool for coming up with the idea.

How was she? What was she doing? Such questions haunted him. Most of all, he tortured himself wondering: would she change her mind? Come January, would she be at the auction house? Six months was starting to feel like a life sentence.

Darcie felt the same way, but she was using the time wisely. Since her return to Buffalo, she'd nailed down several more freelance jobs. The articles she'd written for Nick's auction brochure helped open some doors. Others she unlocked with sheer persistence. Interestingly enough, it was her work as a fact-checker at the trade publication that proved to be the deal sealer when it came to finding full-time employment in New York.

The week before Thanksgiving she interviewed with three magazines in the city, coming into town early on a Friday morning. She'd been tempted to seek out Nick after the interviews were over. His business card was in her purse. But they had a deal. She flew back to Buffalo the following morning, watching the city grow smaller from the plane's tiny window.

Regardless of what happened with Nick, she would be back. Two of the magazines had offered her a job on the spot. Darcie had already called to accept one of them. The pay was low, and she wouldn't be doing as much writing as she'd hoped. At least not at first. But the potential was there in the future not only for assignments, but also for a monthly column in the print magazine as well as in the online version.

In the meantime, she would be living her dream.

Nerves fluttered like a dozen butterflies in her stomach the morning of the auction in January. If all went as she hoped that day, Darcie would be with Nick, and they would be kicking off a new chapter as a couple. In anticipation of that, she made sure to put on her sexiest underwear.

And if he wasn't there?

She pushed the thought away and finished dressing. When she was done, she eyed her reflection in the full-length mirror that was attached to the back of the bathroom door in her tiny Brooklyn efficiency. She had purchased a new dress for the occasion. Red, as she'd promised him. It scooped low in the front and fitted snugly across her hips. When she'd tried it on at the store, she'd snapped a picture with her cell phone and sent it to Becky for confirmation.

Her friend had texted back: Va-va-va-voom.

It was a bit much for a daytime auction, but Darcie didn't care. She wanted to make a statement. And, truth be told, she couldn't wait for Nick to slip it off and then work his way through her sexy undergarments.

The day was cold and it had snowed the night before, leaving the sidewalks covered in slush. After she got out of the cab, she sloshed her way to the auction house's main door in a pair of impractical high heels. Her toes were frozen by the time she got inside the large, cavernous building. She was early by an hour, but the place was already crowded with would-be buyers, car enthusiasts and others who just enjoyed the spectacle. Even though she didn't plan to make any purchases, she had to sign in and received a numbered paddle. Then she made a loop of the main room, hoping to spot Nick. With just minutes to spare before the first automobile went on the block, she hadn't had any luck.

What if he had changed his mind?

She hadn't wanted to consider the possibility, but now, with her nerves working overtime, she could think of little else. Before they'd said goodbye at the airport, he'd seemed so concerned that Darcie would be the one to have second thoughts, given all of the upheaval in her life, but what if he had? What if after six months apart, he'd decided he didn't want to pursue a relationship with her after all?

"Ladies and gentlemen, we'd like to get started. If you could please take your seats," a man's voice said over the public address system.

Darcie found an open spot in the middle of a row halfway up the main aisle.

The first automobile up for bid was an Austin-Healey similar in age to the one Ari had traded to Nick as part of the Porsche deal in Trikala. It needed some body work and the upholstery on the driver's side was in poor condition. It came as no surprise when it went for a song to a man with a handlebar mustache seated three rows behind her.

"Come on now, ladies and gentlemen. You can do better than that," the auctioneer teased the crowd. "These cars are classics. Even the ones that need work are diamonds in the rough."

By the time the fourth automobile came up for bid the crowd was primed. Paddles were shooting into the air all around her, but Darcie had stopped paying attention. She was too busy glancing about for Nick and trying to keep her hopes from deflating.

Maybe she had misunderstood their conversation in the airport. For the third time since arriving at the auction, she looked at the cocktail napkin she'd saved from six months earlier and read the information. There was no mistake. This was the right place. The right time. But where was Nick? Even as she tried to deny it, the answer she kept coming up with was that he'd changed his mind.

Finally, the last vehicle listed in the program came onto the block. It was a 1962 Maserati Spyder. The cherry-red convertible was in mint condition. The auctioneer opened the bidding at seventy-five thousand. It quickly shot up to twice that and kept climbing even as Darcie's spirits started to free-fall.

"I have one-ninety, one-ninety, can I get two? Can I get two?" The auctioneer's chant was rapid-fire. The two in this case referred to two hundred thousand dollars.

The auctioneer got his wish and then some. The vehicle ultimately sold for a quarter of a million dollars. And that was it. The auction was over. Nick wasn't there.

Darcie could barely swallow around the lump in her throat. Her eyes were stinging, her nose starting to run. In a few minutes, she was going to look every bit as wretched as she felt. She wanted to be anywhere but where she was. Unfortunately, leaving wasn't going to be accomplished quickly given the crowd. She rose along with the other people packed in the auditorium. The first tear was sliding down her cheek when the auctioneer's voice boomed over the loudspeaker again.

"Hold on, folks. Hold on. Take your seats again, please. We have one last item up for bid today. It's not listed in your programs. It's something very special."

A murmur of surprise went up from the crowd as people returned to their seats. Darcie swiped at her damp cheeks. Unless she wanted to draw attention to herself by stepping over the half-dozen spectators in her row that were between her and the aisle, she had no choice but to take hers as well.

Once the audience had quieted down, the auctioneer continued. "This item is a little unusual. It's going to require a special buyer, which is why the seller has set a reserve."

Darcie was hunting through her purse for a tissue and only half listening, but she knew that meant the seller had requested a minimum bid be met in order for the sale to go through. Such a strategy could prove risky, but it also ensured that an item of great worth didn't wind up selling way under value simply because the right buyers weren't in attendance.

Must be some car, she thought, momentarily halting her quest for a tissue to glance at the stage. She didn't see an automobile. Instead, she saw Nick saunter out.

The women in the crowd went wild, cheering and clapping and whistling shrilly. Darcie would have joined them had she been capable of making noise. But at that moment, even breathing was proving difficult.

He was here!

And looking gorgeous in a classically cut tuxedo with a snowy white shirt and black bow tie. His dark hair was neatly combed. Just wait till she got him alone. She was going to run her fingers through it, leaving it mussed and sexy.

"I've got a platinum credit card!" a curvy blonde near the front hollered. "Whatever the reserve is, I'm sure I can meet it."

Other women began shouting out dollar amounts then, even though the auctioneer had yet to start the bidding.

"Ladies, ladies. Quiet down. As I said, this is a special auction item. Nick Costas is offering a personal tour of Manhattan and dinner at his favorite Greek restaurant to the woman who meets his reserve."

"What's the amount?" someone called out.

"Nick and I have known one another for a long time.

We're competitors in business, but friends, too. Still, he hasn't told me. All he has said is that he will let me know when or if the terms of the sale have been met."

When the audience began grumbling, the auctioneer silenced them. "It gets more bizarre, folks. Nick will pick up the tab for the winning bid and give the amount to the charity of the winner's choice."

"So, there's no risk?" a woman asked.

"Only to your hearts. So, ladies, get ready to raise those paddles. Bidding starts at one thousand dollars."

It escalated quickly from there, hitting ten thousand before Darcie could process what was happening. He was selling himself, but not to the highest bidder. That was where the reserve came in. Nick was waiting for her. If she loved him, he was, quite literally, hers for the taking.

Darcie set her paddle on her seat. She didn't need it. She had a better idea.

"Excuse me," she said to the gentleman seated to her left. She had to repeat the process five more times before she made it to the aisle and was heading toward the stage. She no longer cared about making a spectacle of herself.

Nick spotted her when she was halfway there. His mouth curved into a grin that set her heart bumping irregularly.

"I believe the reserve has been met," he told the auctioneer. His gaze never wavered from hers.

She climbed the steps and met him center stage. The huge crowd fell silent. For Darcie, at that moment, they simply didn't exist.

"I was getting a little worried that you weren't here," she admitted, wrapping her arms around his neck.

His hands found her waist. "I apologize for that. I wanted to make a statement."

"You certainly did. I was going for that with this dress, by the way."

"So I see. I can't wait to take it off you. Six months is very long."

"Felt like a lifetime," she agreed. "But I've kept busy."

"Writing?" he asked.

"And plenty of it. Did I mention I moved here to take a job at a magazine? I just started last week."

His smile was wide and tinged with pride. "I knew you could do it."

"Kiss him already!" the woman who'd offered her credit card at the beginning of the auction shouted.

Darcie grinned. "How do you feel about public displays of affection?"

In answer, Nick lowered his mouth to hers.

"I love you, Darcie Hayes," he whispered afterward.

"I love you, too."

EPILOGUE

BECKY FUSSED WITH the satin folds of Darcie's wedding gown as they stood at the back of the church. Although the denomination wasn't Greek Orthodox, much to Yiayia's dismay, Darcie had insisted that some of the elements of a traditional Greek ceremony be incorporated into their wedding.

One year to the day after they'd met in the Athens airport, Nick had gotten down on one knee and proposed. Now, Darcie was minutes away from becoming his wife.

The music began. Her sisters, wearing dresses the same shade of blue as the Aegean, started up the aisle one at a time. As Darcie's maid of honor, Becky went last. Then it was just Darcie and her father standing at the back of the church, a white runner strewn with rose petals the only thing between her and Nick.

"Slow down," her father whispered, as they began to walk as the wedding march began. "Make him wait a little longer."

It might have been good advice if Darcie had not been so eager herself. She already felt as if she'd waited a lifetime for this moment, even if by many standards her romance with Nick had been a whirlwind.

Finally at the altar, she smiled at Nick, took his hands. Vows were spoken. Rings were exchanged. A unity candle was lit. Then Pieter, grinning broadly, placed crowns on their heads and switched them three times.

"You may kiss your bride," the priest said.

Nick's eyes were bright. His expression mirrored the sheer joy Darcie felt.

"At last," he murmured just before their mouths met.

* * * * *

Mills & Boon® Hardback
September 2013

ROMANCE

Challenging Dante	Lynne Graham
Captivated by Her Innocence	Kim Lawrence
Lost to the Desert Warrior	Sarah Morgan
His Unexpected Legacy	Chantelle Shaw
Never Say No to a Caffarelli	Melanie Milburne
His Ring Is Not Enough	Maisey Yates
A Reputation to Uphold	Victoria Parker
A Whisper of Disgrace	Sharon Kendrick
If You Can't Stand the Heat...	Joss Wood
Maid of Dishonour	Heidi Rice
Bound by a Baby	Kate Hardy
In the Line of Duty	Ami Weaver
Patchwork Family in the Outback	Soraya Lane
Stranded with the Tycoon	Sophie Pembroke
The Rebound Guy	Fiona Harper
Greek for Beginners	Jackie Braun
A Child to Heal Their Hearts	Dianne Drake
Sheltered by Her Top-Notch Boss	Joanna Neil

MEDICAL

The Wife He Never Forgot	Anne Fraser
The Lone Wolf's Craving	Tina Beckett
Re-awakening His Shy Nurse	Annie Claydon
Safe in His Hands	Amy Ruttan

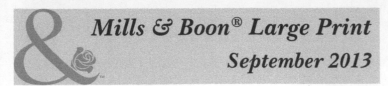

Mills & Boon® Large Print
September 2013

ROMANCE

A Rich Man's Whim	Lynne Graham
A Price Worth Paying?	Trish Morey
A Touch of Notoriety	Carole Mortimer
The Secret Casella Baby	Cathy Williams
Maid for Montero	Kim Lawrence
Captive in his Castle	Chantelle Shaw
Heir to a Dark Inheritance	Maisey Yates
Anything but Vanilla...	Liz Fielding
A Father for Her Triplets	Susan Meier
Second Chance with the Rebel	Cara Colter
First Comes Baby...	Michelle Douglas

HISTORICAL

The Greatest of Sins	Christine Merrill
Tarnished Amongst the Ton	Louise Allen
The Beauty Within	Marguerite Kaye
The Devil Claims a Wife	Helen Dickson
The Scarred Earl	Elizabeth Beacon

MEDICAL

NYC Angels: Redeeming The Playboy	Carol Marinelli
NYC Angels: Heiress's Baby Scandal	Janice Lynn
St Piran's: The Wedding!	Alison Roberts
Sydney Harbour Hospital: Evie's Bombshell	Amy Andrews
The Prince Who Charmed Her	Fiona McArthur
His Hidden American Beauty	Connie Cox

Mills & Boon® Hardback

October 2013

ROMANCE

The Greek's Marriage Bargain	Sharon Kendrick
An Enticing Debt to Pay	Annie West
The Playboy of Puerto Banús	Carol Marinelli
Marriage Made of Secrets	Maya Blake
Never Underestimate a Caffarelli	Melanie Milburne
The Divorce Party	Jennifer Hayward
A Hint of Scandal	Tara Pammi
A Façade to Shatter	Lynn Raye Harris
Whose Bed Is It Anyway?	Natalie Anderson
Last Groom Standing	Kimberly Lang
Single Dad's Christmas Miracle	Susan Meier
Snowbound with the Soldier	Jennifer Faye
The Redemption of Rico D'Angelo	Michelle Douglas
The Christmas Baby Surprise	Shirley Jump
Backstage with Her Ex	Louisa George
Blame It on the Champagne	Nina Harrington
Christmas Magic in Heatherdale	Abigail Gordon
The Motherhood Mix-Up	Jennifer Taylor

MEDICAL

Gold Coast Angels: A Doctor's Redemption	Marion Lennox
Gold Coast Angels: Two Tiny Heartbeats	Fiona McArthur
The Secret Between Them	Lucy Clark
Craving Her Rough Diamond Doc	Amalie Berlin

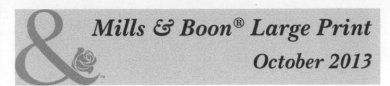

Mills & Boon® Large Print

October 2013

ROMANCE

HISTORICAL

MEDICAL